Stone of Doubt

by

Margaret Izard

Stones of Iona

Cover Art by *Lisa Dawn MacDonald*

The Wild Rose Press, Inc.
PO Box 708
Adams Basin, NY 14410-0708
Visit us at www.thewildrosepress.com

Publishing History
First Edition, 2025
Trade Paperback ISBN 978-1-5092-6077-5
Digital ISBN 978-1-5092-6076-8

Stones of Iona
Published in the United States of America

Dedication

To my husband, thank you for all your love and support. Thank you for putting up with your oddball wife and all my quirky goodness. Every day is an adventure!

Chapter 1

"Don't ever doubt yourselves or waste a second of your life. It's too short, and you're too special."

The graduation speaker's voice echoed in her mind. Doubt, it's what she'd done most of her life—doubted herself, her abilities. Evie MacDougall should have been excited like the rest of her graduating class, but she wasn't in the moment. The American pop star the college had invited to speak at Edinburgh's College of Performing Arts Studio Scotland was a great singer but desperately skinny. Evie wondered if the woman ever ate. She tried to diet once, but Kat MacArthur, her best friend, always told her she had nothing to worry about. Guys loved curvy women. Well, she was definitely curvaceous like her ma. Kat swore Evie turned all the heads of the boys at school. Still, under her graduation gown, she wore a black baggy dress hiding her curves. The color matched her dyed hair. Black from her chestnut brown, like her mom's, and her typical black eye liner. She'd promised her ma no black lipstick for graduation. But if she'd had her choice, she'd be decked out in her typical goth look.

Her twin brother Ewan elbowed her. "Ye ready for our walk across the stage? The prank?"

Evie rolled her eyes. "Aye, like Ma's graduation from Rice University in the States, where the mascot's handler held the live owl under his robes until he

1

walked across the stage. When he hit center stage, he held it up with the bird's wings flapping."

Ewan chuckled. "I always wondered how he managed it without the bird shitting on him."

Evie snorted. "Well, with ours, it won't be a live animal. So ye won't have to worry about it." Brigid, the MacDougall Fae, was assigned to assist the family in protecting the magic stones of Iona, powerful Fae stones, and gifted her and her brother with Fae powers when they were young. Now, almost twenty-four, the forces grew, manifesting differently for each twin. Evie's powers centered on emotions—like the powers surrounding people—while Ewan's centered more on human minds.

The pop singer's voice carried across McEwan Hall as she spoke in a sing-songy tone. "Happy Graduation, class of 2022!"

Her classmates stood and cheered. Evie clapped but didn't hold the same enthusiasm. As they lined up to receive their diplomas, Evie grunted. The actual documents wouldn't arrive until much later at their family's home, Dunstaffnage Castle in Argyle, Scotland. Today, each graduate received a rolled blank paper with a red ribbon—still the symbol of success and progression. For Evie, it rang short. In all her jaunts into some of the most haunted places in Edinburgh, one of the most haunted cities in Scotland, she'd yet to capture a ghost on film. Oh, she saw plenty, thanks to her gift of Fae abilities. But to get one on film would surely land her in the *Photographic Journalism Magazine of Scotland*.

Ewan poked her from behind. "Evie, pay attention, they called Jessie MacDonald. MacDougall is next. Ye need to cross the stage and set yer energy up for me to project off of to get our animal glowing."

She whispered over her shoulder, "I know, ye bampot."

George MacEwan murmured from behind Ewan, "Ye both going to pull a prank again? The last one nearly got ye both sent packing."

Ewan laughed. "Aye, well, nothing like going out with a bang!"

The Dean of the Performing Arts Studio Scotland, Professor Ford, a jolly, heavy-set man, stood holding a scroll, awaiting Evie to cross the stage.

The announcer, his assistant, Mary, spoke into the microphone. "Evie MacDougall."

Evie strode forward and took her scroll as Professor Ford turned them for the photographer to snap a shot. Evie smiled and walked to the end of the stage. She turned and twisted her wrist, flinging her free hand out to place a wall of energy over the students seated on the main floor.

Ewan threw both hands out, casting the spirit of their chosen animal to project its shape across the energy curtain. As the majestic animal formed, the speaker gasped into the microphone.

****

As the speaker called Evie's name, Brielle MacDougall gripped her husband and true love's hand tightly. "This is it, Colin. Our babies graduate."

Colin lifted her hand to his lips, kissing the back. "Aye, Bree, but ye grip my hand any harder, ye might break it."

When her daughter reached the end of the stage and turned, Bree whispered, "You don't think the twins will pull another prank, do you?"

Colin grumbled as Bree sensed the energy shift in the room. A signal her children gathered natural energy for a Fae spell. Evie flicked her wrist, a movement most wouldn't notice, but being her mother, Bree recognized the action. Her gaze shot at her son on the opposite side of the stage as he lifted both arms.

Bree hissed, "They wouldn't!"

Bright lights danced over the graduates seated on the main level as a unicorn made of white, yellow, and blue illuminations galloped over their heads. As it disappeared, a loud whinny echoed across the hall.

The crowd gasped as the students stood and cheered. "MacDougall, MacDougall, MacDougall."

Colin growled, "Damn them. That was impressive."

Bree patted his hand. "Well, at least this time, the Dean of the College can't threaten to expel them. They graduate today."

As the students quieted, the speaker cleared her throat and spoke into the microphone. "Ewan McDougall." Her son strode across the stage, took his scroll, and stopped for a picture as he posed, standing tall. The Dean whispered into his ear, and Ewan roared with laughter as he walked away. Dean Ford laughed as well. Well, at least this was the last of their college antics.

Her eyes teared as the moment overwhelmed her.

She sniffled as Colin leaned over. "Dry yer tears. This is a great time. Yer wee bugs are all grown up."

They had, and quite well.

****

Ewan joined Evie as they walked back to their

seats. "Did ye see it? The entire graduating class will talk about it for years to come!"

As she sat, Evie didn't quite feel the same excitement her brother did. The spell conjuring the unicorn, an easy one, still set her on edge. While unicorns were considered mythical in the human realm, Brigid had told her, in the Fae realm, they truly existed as revered animals with their own magic.

The memory of her Fae boy, Aodhán, from years ago came to her as it often did, especially now that she embarked upon a new chapter in her life, graduating college.

****

He was tall with light, almost white hair and had a boyish, good-looking face, like a model, and dressed in all white, like Brigid. When she'd glanced again, he winked at her.

The boy leaned back next to her and gazed out the window as he whispered in her ear, "There once was a Fae. A Fae prince born as grandson to the great king of the good Fae, the Tuatha Dé Danann. His mother and father rejoiced at the birth of their son with exceptional gifts that few Fae have."

Evie exhaled. "What gifts?"

The boy's grin came through in the tone of his response. "Some powerful, some sweet, some scary. The power he held was vast. He trained in his youth to control these powers, since they could cause great harm if misused."

Evie looked at him, and he smiled. "The Fae boy, he had many dreams. Some made sense, and some did not. One dream, in particular, was of a girl. A human girl."

Evie blushed and gazed at their hands. He caressed hers as he held it. "When he woke, he couldn't remember what the girl looked like, only how she made him feel."

Evie peeked at his face. "How did she make him feel?"

The boy sighed. "Tingly, warm, happy. Whole." The boy frowned and glanced at their hands. "He knew how she made him feel but could never see her face. His mother, a powerful Fae, searched the land far and wide to find his dream girl. She never found her. His father searched as well, to no avail."

Evie stared as the boy peeked up at her. "It wasn't until he had a vision of her through the Eye of Ra that he saw her face for the first time. Then he knew who she was." He leaned in, their faces close.

Evie whispered, "Who was she?"

The boy replied, "The girl of his dreams."

He kissed her lightly on the lips. Holding her hand in his, he slid his other hand around her and pulled her closer, holding her in his embrace. He kissed her again, this time deeper.

A boy had kissed Evie once, but it was wet and flat. This soft, warm kiss stirred her as they breathed together. Butterflies fluttered in her chest, and her stomach did a flip.

Evie gasped, and the boy slid his tongue into her mouth. She was light and hot at once as she eagerly returned his kisses.

He slowly ended the kiss and held Evie as they lounged together, watching the land at night speed by.

After some time, the boy sat up, staring at the door, then turned to Evie. "I must go. Someone comes."

Evie let out a whimper. She didn't want him to go.

He peered at her, and she sensed he didn't want to leave.

With a twist of his wrist, a ball of light formed. He shifted, handing it to her.

She watched the light, mesmerized.

He spoke, breaking the spell. "Take the light, Evie."

She held her hand out, and he carefully placed the small ball of light into her hand. It warmed, like when he held her hand. She sighed in wonder.

"Close yer hand around it and place it by yer heart."

Evie did so, and it warmed her body as the light faded.

"When ye want to call me to ye, think of me. Twist yer wrist as I did, and the light will glow. I will come at yer call."

****

She sighed as Ewan elbowed her. "Come on, Evie girl, cheer up. We graduated!"

Evie shrugged as Ewan leaned over, whispering, "Ye still aren't pining for that Fae guy from the trip to Egypt, are ye?"

She shook her head and sat quietly as the rest of their class walked across the stage. She put her feelings aside—pining for a boy she hadn't seen in nearly eight years. Ewan had said it was a waste of time, but her heart wouldn't stop aching. *Aodhán.*

"Manix Skene." Evie's head came up as Manix crossed the stage. Since he transferred, she'd eyed him from afar in the last three months. He was a drama major who preferred goth, like her, and carried darkness about him all the girls found irresistible.

As Manix turned and posed for his graduation picture, Jessie MacDonald sighed. "What I wouldn't give for a date with Manix, The Warlock himself."

Evie snorted—warlock, indeed. Manix was as much Fae as Jessie. Brigid had warned her and her brother that warlocks were evil Fae and to avoid their dark magic at all costs. Evie sat forward as Manix strode off the stage. Still, his portrayal in the play he'd written for his graduation project was darkly attractive.

Evie wondered what being with a dark and forbidding man like Manix would be like. Would he love her deeply and obsess over her, like the way the telly portrayed vampires?

Ewan elbowed her again. "That's the last one. 'Tis almost time to toss yer cap."

Evie must have zoned out for a while. After Manix, there were at least twenty more graduates.

Evie stood and tossed her cap with the rest of her class, a signal that the time had come to move on. Aodhán wasn't coming back. Maybe it was time to let go of her mystery Fae boy, her lost love.

She caught her cap as Ewan grabbed her hand. "Come, shift us to Ma and Da. I'm starved, and they promised to take us to eat."

Evie pulled back her hand as her brother stopped.

She raised an eyebrow, and Ewan smirked. "Ye shift us to them but not obvious. If they discover we used more magic, I won't get a free lunch!"

She closed her eyes as she held Ewan's hand and thought of her parents, the only set of humans who loved her unconditionally. The world tilted a bit, turned a little, and dizziness overcame her. Her world righted again. She opened her eyes, the crowd parted, and she and Ewan stood before the couple.

Her da, Colin, pointed a finger with a raised eyebrow as her mother, Bree, rushed to her, hugging her. "Oh, my wee bugs!" She hugged her brother next, who kissed his ma's cheek as she exclaimed, "I'm so proud of you!"

Their da walked to them with his finger shaking. "Ye both are lucky this is yer last day."

Ewan grinned wide. "Aye, Da. Let's get to the pub. I'm ready for a burger and a pint."

Colin smiled back. "Ye are always ready to eat. But aye, celebrations are in order, and a pint will suit me just fine. We'll meet John, Marie, Doug, and Kat MacArthur there." John was the captain of Dunstaffnage Castle and practically her father's shadow. Marie and John's kids were Doug and Kat— Evie's best friend.

Her ma took her arm in hers as the group strode out of McEwan Hall and turned, heading to the Garden District. "A short walk, and we shall be there. Ye work tonight?"

Evie shook her head. "No. The South Bridge Vault Vigil is tonight. I told ye about it."

Ewan turned, glancing over his shoulder. "She's still chasing ghosts, Ma."

Evie tugged on his graduation gown's cowl, making him choke. "Yeah, and all I need to be famous is to capture one on film."

Ewan's powers centered on minds, and hers centered on emotions, making sensing people's spirits easier. She saw many ghosts all the time, especially in Edinburgh. Some spoke to her, like Maggie Dickson —

an infamous character in Edinburgh's history who stayed around a pub named after her in the Garden District of Edinburgh. They'd hung her just outside the very building, and her family thought her dead until they got halfway home. Maggie sat up, scaring her relatives and everyone around her. Evie never understood why her spirit hadn't moved on. She'd lived a full life after, married, had kids, and died a happy woman. Yet her soul still lingered, unable to find peace.

As their group approached, her ghost friend stood outside. Evie's da and brother passed the apparition.

Her ma did as well, but Evie stopped. "Hi, Maggie."

The form waved in and out like a candle. "Evie. Ye aren't working the pub this evening?"

Evie shook her head. "No, I'm going to South Street, the vaults."

Maggie lifted and lowered like a breeze. "There's a strangeness about tonight, Evie. I'd be careful if I were ye."

A group of college kids Evie knew well ran by, all dressed in graduation robes. They were some drama majors with part-time jobs playing the part of graduates from a wizard school, mimicking that wizard movie for the tourists. They did this daily. A jog down Victoria Street turned onto Grassmarket Street and by her workplace. Victoria Street, with its colorful buildings, crooked architecture, and unique shops, evoked a sense of magic and whimsy, as it was the inspiration for a hidden magical alley where the wizards from the movie purchased magic supplies. The street alone drew tourists by the hundreds each day.

Anne called out as they ran by. "Look, it's Evie

MacDougall! Ye see any spirits yet?"

Evie turned away as Anne approached. Maggie stuck her foot out. A burst of energy came from her, making her foot solid, tripping Anne as she came by.

Anne face-planted on the pavement.

She quickly stood. "Evie, that wasn't funny."

Evie shrugged. "It was a ghostie, I promise."

A girl with Anne, Ria, took her hand as she called out to Evie. "Weirdo!"

Maggie giggled, and Evie snorted a laugh when the women walked away.

"Ye shouldn't tease them, ye know." The man's voice rumbled from her left. She turned and came face to face with Manix Skene. *It was him!*

Evie turned to Maggie to make a face about the handsome, mysterious boy who finally paid her any attention, and Maggie had disappeared. Gone.

As she felt Manix move closer, she turned back. He towered over her at over six feet, and his jet-black hair gleamed in the sun. Now that she was close, it was darker than hers. His scent came to her, heady musk that set her nerves on edge.

He grinned as he spoke, "That trick ye pulled at graduation with yer brother. Magic?"

Evie laughed, but it came out as a hiccup, "No, hidden projectors." Did he know? No one ever suspected the real magic they'd used for pranks.

Manix gazed at her with a smile. "An interesting choice for yer animal. A unicorn." He hummed. "Mythical yet powerful. An elusive creature. Yet if one were to capture her, dominate her, use her powers to gain control." He huffed, "That would be something."

Evie blinked. "Yes, well, as I said. Projectors."

They stood in awkward silence for a moment. Evie spied Manix many times on his way to work. He used his talents as an actor, giving wizard movie tours for tourists in the Greyfriars Kirkyard. In his robes from graduation, he looked ready to work.

Evie fumbled with her robes. "Ye meeting anyone for a celebration for graduating?"

Manix shook his head. "No, I have to work."

Evie waved her hand to the side. "I saw ye in the play from Glow." Glow was the arts cumulative display of artists graduating that year. His warlock play was a hit among all the women.

At Manix's grin, Evie brightened. "The self-written and directed play ye stared in, *Lies of the Warlock.* It was very good." Manix played the warlock disguised as a mutant living among humans. His portrayal of the man's painful and horrific journey of discovery exposed a deeper pain in the character with dark, demonic undertones. Evie found it dramatically appealing.

Manix stepped closer. "I saw yer work, *Out of the Blue,* in Drill Hall." His hand brushed her arm. "Yer work is extraordinary."

Evie blushed. Her series of photos of Loch Evie in varying stages of sunrise and sunset that captured the different tones of blue was very personal to her—the beauty of her home, Glen Etive.

Her ma called from inside the pub, "Evie, come on! Yer brother and father are so hungry they might eat the menu!"

Evie glanced inside, not wanting to leave Manix's side now that he'd finally noticed her and had spoken to her—a boy she'd secretly wanted to meet since he arrived at college months ago.

Manix took her hand in his. "Ye go on to yer celebration."

He brought it to his lips, his breath teasing her skin. "We can continue this over dinner tomorrow night."

Her breath left her in anticipation of his kiss. Her heart beat hard.

He brushed a light kiss. "Seven at Devil's Advocate Bar." Her ears rang. He'd asked her out!

He rubbed his thumb over the tingling area. "Come dressed to impress."

As he let go of her hand, she sucked in a breath. "Should I give ye my cell number?"

Manix smiled. "I don't have a cell. Don't need it." He strode away, confident in his steps.

Her mother approached and stood beside her. "Who was that?"

Evie's knees nearly gave out as she sighed his name, "Manix."

Her ma hummed, "What happened to the Fae boy?"

Manix turned and winked at her as she spoke. "What Fae boy?"

Bree's eyes followed hers to Manix's. "Well, now I see what you mean. Dashing man. New friend?"

A new friend indeed. Evie felt like she'd stepped out of the darkness she'd waited in for so long; years of longing for a boy who broke his promise and never returned now seemed wasted. Evie vowed then and there never to seek the Fae boy again. It was time. Today started a new chapter in her life, one she planned on living.

Evie turned to her ma and smirked. "Maybe." She

walked into the pub and called over her shoulder, "Come on, Ma. Ye said Ewan and Da were hungry."

Chapter 2

Kat flopped onto Evie's bed, jostling her camera equipment. Kat's compact yet full body jiggled in her revealing crop top outfit and short flare shorts, looking like a skirt. How Kat ever felt comfortable showing so much skin was beyond Evie's comprehension. She stood there comfortably in her loose torn jeans and black baggy tee-shirt with her long black hair in a ponytail. Her gothic looks were complete with black nail polish, kohl eyeliner, and lipstick.

Evie grabbed her digital camera before it fell off the bed. "Careful, Kitkat." Evie rechecked the settings and placed the camera into her bag with an assortment of lenses, another digital camera with infrared, and her older trusty film camera. All cleaned and ready for an evening of catching ghosts. She eyed her friend. Kat was their nickname for her, her formal name being Katheryn MacArthur.

Kat rolled over, placing her elbows on the bed and her head in her hands. "I can't believe I'm finally here." She rolled on her back, her arms going wide. "At college! Away from ma, away from chores, away on an adventure!"

Evie laughed. "Not even here a day, and ye think ye are on vacation." She pointed her finger at her BFF since childhood. "Chores still exist, and this week, yers is cleaning the loo."

Kat shrugged. "So, I have things to do. At least it's not a constant upkeep like the priory. My ma's obsessed with the old pile of holy rocks." Years ago, after Doug and Kat's parents married, they moved into the old Ardchattan Priory near Dunstaffnage Castle, fulfilling Kat's ma's dream of renovating a religious building. They live in it to this day.

Kat hummed. "Summer classes start soon, and I'm happy I'm not stuck in some dorm but here in yer flat." She sighed. "Our flat."

"Not just ours; Doug and Ewan's as well." Douglas MacArthur was her brother's best friend and Kat's older brother. Both were the children of the Captain of Dunstaffnage Castle, John MacArthur, Evie's da's close friend and assistant.

Evie checked her camera once again, making sure she'd fully charged the battery. "Aye, I suppose ye have yer da to thank for getting to come now. Graduating early, finishing at the top of yer class. His studies in physics helping ye since he tutored ye."

Kat sat up and straightened her top. "Aye, well, the college has yet to experience my knowledge."

Evie rolled her eyes. "Don't be surprised if ye don't dazzle the professors."

Kat tilted her head. "Yer ghosts. I am convinced they travel between realms, using energy much the same way Fae portals do. Like the fifth and sixth rule of Superstring Theory."

Kat folded her hand as if she held a crystal ball. "In the fifth theory, we would see a world slightly different from our own that would give us a means of measuring the similarity and differences between our world and other possible ones."

She rolled her hands over and folded them flat, opening them as if revealing a new world. "Then in the sixth, we would see a plane of potential worlds, where we could compare and position all the viable universes that start with the same initial conditions as this one, like The Big Bang."

Kat smiled as she held her hands out. "In theory, if you could master the fifth and sixth dimensions, you could travel back in time or go to different futures provided you had a means of transport, like a black hole. I believe the ghosts do the same."

Evie chuckled. "When ye start in on yer physics talk, all I hear is blah, blah, blah!"

Kat laid back on the pillows, tossing her arms wide. "Blah, blah, nothing. Ye said Manix asked ye out. The one boy ye lusted after from afar. Even when ye committed yerself to Aodhán, yer Fae love."

Evie turned to her closet to grab her coat. Thankfully, the action hid her face from Kat. Being best friends, Kat would have likely caught the expression of pain cross her face at the mention of Aodhán, even if just today she'd committed to not seek him out again via the Fae ball of energy he'd gifted her. She paused, leaving him forever, still hurt.

When she turned back, she plastered a grin on her face. "Aye, a date with a new man." She flung on her coat. "But first, I go to capture pictures of the dead."

Kat picked at the pillow. "Evie, did ye ever wonder why ye weren't meant to photograph ghosts if ye can really see them?" She sat forward. "Maybe it's like a power they have. They show themselves to ye since ye can see them but refuse to give ye any proof. But those of us who can't see them, they give hints to, in pictures."

Kat glanced up at her. "They come to ye for help, advice."

The image of Dunstaffnage Castle's Green Lady flashed in Evie's mind. Her forlorn expression was clear, but no tears. The last time she'd seen her, another younger woman in different age clothing stood behind her, both sad and waiting, but for what?

Her eyes met Kat's knowing expression. "The Green Lady. Ye saw her last time ye were at the castle, didn't ye?" Kat asked.

Evie shrugged on her coat. "Aye, what of it? I see her all the time."

Kat hugged her knees to her. "She cried?"

Evie shook her head, "No, she's never cried for me."

Kat spoke lowly, "But she hasn't smiled either."

Evie slung her bag over her shoulder. "No. This last time, there was another with her, younger and with more modern clothing. Old still, but not like the lady. They wait, but for what I can't tell."

As Kat spoke, Evie strode to the door. "But each time ye take a pic, they aren't there."

Evie stopped at the door. "Aye, it's the same with all ghosts."

Kat sat up. "Well, I hope tonight is different for ye. Cast doubt from yer mind and believe."

Doubt. Evie merely nodded and pushed through the door.

****

The walk to Edinburgh South Bridge and The Vaults gave Evie plenty of time to gather her thoughts.

"Cast doubt from yer mind." She blew a laugh. Kat

almost sounded like one of the Fae fables from the *Fae Fable Book*. The book given to MacDougall by the Fae held stories that told the fate of each magic Iona Stone. Some fables were proven true over the years, as the Fae called upon the MacDougalls to hunt a magic stone lost in space and time and return it to the Fae before the evil Fae got their greedy hands on one, throwing the realms into chaos. She'd seen only one, the Stone of Hope, a green rectangular stone they'd found in a statue in Egypt, the Valley of the Kings, when her uncle, Dominic DeVolt, met his true love, Moira. That was in the past, the 1930s, but now they live in the present in Florida. Her cousin's cherub face flashed in her mind from the last visit. Annie was an energized child with flaming red hair brighter than her mother's.

Evie bumped into a man who turned. "Pardon me, miss. Ye here for the ghost tours?"

Evie nodded. It seemed she'd come upon the crowd without noticing, chiding herself for wool-gathering.

A voice she recognized boomed over the crowd, "Welcome to our very special overnight tour called "Vaults Vigils" where we open the doors of the vaults to the general public every Friday night from midnight until dawn."

The man's gaze roamed the crowd. Evie had met George, who studied history at her college, before. His dramatic flair when leading the vault tours always entertained Evie.

George's voice rose as he spoke, "Ye intrepid souls will be given the chance to brave the Blair Street vaults with a trained Mercat Guide"—he pointed to himself—"and showed how to use the latest ghost hunting equipment. Electric magnetic field recorders and infrared thermometers will be made available to small groups who will conduct a series of controlled experiments with the chance to compare and contrast results at the end of the evening." Murmurs traveled the crowd, their nervous energy built in anticipation of seeing a real ghost. Evie's climbed with them even though she'd been here many times. Each time, she still got butterflies in her belly.

George called out again, "Break into yer groups, and we'll get started."

Out of pure habit, Evie stepped aside, calling upon her inner energy when she neared the vault entrance, before she remembered she'd vowed never to call Aodhán again. She hesitated but flicked her wrist, calling Aodhán's ball of energy. The ball appeared in her hand but didn't glow. Deep down, she'd hoped trying again outside the vaults might make him appear, since the veil between realms thinned here. As in her many attempts before, the ball didn't glow, and Aodhán, her Fae love, didn't appear.

George tapped her shoulder. "Ye going it alone again?"

Without turning, Evie nodded as she folded her hand into her chest. The ball disappeared inside her hand. She pulled her camera from her bag, placed the strap over her head, and followed the last group into the vaults where, centuries before, the underbelly of Edinburgh's poorest people lived.

As groups progressed through the underground tunnels, their equipment flashed and whined as ghosts floated past them. Not a single human saw them, but Evie did. As usual, there were so many ghosts. Some were in a permanent state of illness. Some starved to their deaths. One hacked a cough. Evie snapped shots here and there as she tried to capture anything on film.

A ghost she'd not seen here before tapped her shoulder. "Please help me. I want to be free." A man in rags, skinny and ailing, met her observation. The aura surrounding him was blue. A sense of power and insightfulness came from him. No evil, just another lost soul in this realm. If she cast energy around him, the space would open, and energy would transport him to what the humans knew as heaven. Evie stared into his eyes as they pleaded for escape. The blackness in an aura that showed hell did not appear around him. Evie felt comfortable helping this one soul.

She nodded and pulled on her Fae energy to open a hole in the realm. She shifted her hand and cast energy around his spirit.

A shaft of light shone from above. As it opened, people, likely his friends and family, stood with hands outstretched, welcoming him and calling him to come to the light.

As the man floated toward it, he glanced over his shoulder. "Thank ye, angel."

Evie lifted her camera, holding the button and snapping multiple pics. The light faded, and the tunnel grew dim. So many, so desperate to ease their suffering.

She turned the corner, and a group of women ghosts disappeared. Why some dodged her at times, she didn't know.

A child drifted past, floating in the tunnel. "My doll. Where's my doll?"

A woman in the group before Evie bent and set a figure on the ground. The apparition floated there, grabbed the doll, and flew past Evie, who lifted her camera as it clicked with multiple pics.

Evie had seen the ghost child before, one who died a painful death from illness and always searched for her lost doll. Sometimes, she appeared before humans, so one in the group always brought a doll. The more people saw the spirit, the more the child's story gained popularity, resulting in, at a minimum, a doll each tour. Where the ghost placed all those dolls was a mystery to Evie.

George called everyone to the entrance. "Come, let's gather outside and compare findings."

As Evie proceeded out the vault's door, he called to her, "Any pics tonight, Evie?" Evie lifted her camera and flicked through the pics, but not one showed the ghosts she'd seen. Every picture was bare except for the live humans. She shook her head and stepped out.

George called back, "Maybe next time?"

Evie waved and progressed down the street a bit, stopping to lean against the lamp post, allowing the circle of light to comfort her.

Kat's claim from earlier echoed in her mind, *"Evie, did ye ever wonder that ye weren't meant to photograph ghosts if ye can really see them?"*

A human who saw ghosts, yet she wasn't permitted to photograph one for proof. The irony had not escaped her. The Fae were like that sometimes. Her family Fae, Brigid, was the best at tricks, reminding Evie of the many stunts she'd played on Evie and her brother's minds. Brigid claimed they kept them smart and aware. But Evie sensed Brigid enjoyed the game.

A group from the tour ambled past, their excited voices carrying in the night. "Did ye see it? The girl with the doll."

A woman replied, "Aye, took the doll and disappeared."

Evie huffed, "Damn it, and I didn't get a pic."

She stood there wondering if she'd ever get the image of a ghost.

****

The sphere called him, much as before, but today, finally freed from his punishment, Aodhán's excitement grew. This was the first time he'd be able to respond to the repeated calls from the energy ball he'd given Evie MacDougall those many human years ago.

He sat in his bedroom in his grandfather's castle in the Fae realm. The Tuatha Dé Danann king's seat, Broemere Castle, glittered as its blue Fae crystal reflected the sunlight. The fortress, constructed at the beginning of time, sat on the ridge of Broemere, a spiritual location for the Fae. In the distance, the sea glittered beyond the rise as a dragon flew overhead.

Recently released from imprisonment for showing Evie MacDougall multiple spells forbidden for humans, Aodhán experienced the first call from the sphere while he could answer.

His mother, Brigid, the MacDougall Fae, strode into his room. "Aodhán, I sense it as well. Ye cannot go running off at her first call."

His mother crossed to him and ruffled his hair as he dodged the gesture from his youth. "Mother, I've waited too long. Nine human years feels like an eternity when ye can't go to the one ye love."

Brigid sat beside him, a floating pillow of clouds, yet as firm as each owner needed. "Son, ye are a Fae prince, grandson to the great king of the Good Fae, the Tuatha Dé Danann. Ye hold the most exceptional gifts that few Fae have. But ye in the human world, I fear for what ye shall face."

She patted his hand. "The new king of Fomoire, he is powerful as well. And so many unknowns about him other than his unpredictable temperament."

True, the recent battle where the new king of the evil Fae had tried to take over the Tuatha Dé Danann flashed in his mind. The pain of losing his father hit hard. The new king had come into his title by force due to his claim of heredity, being Balor's son. They'd crowned him the next king even though he'd met opposition from many in the Fomoire kingdom. All questioned the youth's origins but got no direct answers. The new king's short temper took out half an entire fighting force of Fae, adding another crime to his growing list. First, the attack on the good Fae kingdom in an attempted takeover, then the killing of fellow Fae. The new king's reputation had grown. And now, he'd vanished, avoiding facing the Fae council for his crimes.

Aodhán stood and paced. Over the years, his boyish body grew into his immortal being. Tall, muscular, and that of a warrior more hardened for physical warfare than the hexes and spells the Fae used in battle. While isolated, physical activity kept the boredom at bay, since the Fae Council forbade him to use any of his Fae powers.

He turned on his mother. "A Fae fable has shown itself. I know it's Evie. I feel it in my heart."

He sighed. "The quote, 'There is a sacredness in tears. They are not the mark of weakness but of power. The power of tears shall quell any person.' It must mean her."

Brigid stood and crossed to him. "In this, ye may be right. Yer powers are much stronger than most, even than yer grandfather Dagda, king of the Tuatha Dé Danann. But take care, for yer mom's worried heart."

Aodhán hugged and kissed his mother. "I have no doubts, Mother, Evie is my soul mate. I must go. She needs me."

He turned to the wall as the clouds parted, revealing a seeing portal where a Fae could gaze into any realm on a command. Aodhán closed his eyes and called to Evie. His heart swelled with love, fluttered a little, then centered on Evie's aura of pure pink. Evie's kindness, care, and love washed over him. She tracked ghosts of all things. As she carried a camera, she looked mature.

Well, he'd grown as well.

Her grace showed through, even in her baggy dark clothing. She turned, and he had his first view of her face. Still heart-shaped, but longer; youth's fullness had grown into a young woman's beauty.

His heart skipped as he devised the best way to appear to his love for the first time in so many human years. *Surprise her* popped into his mind.

He flicked his wrist, opened a portal to the human realm, and faded from his Fae realm.

As his last waves left Broemere Castle, his mother whispered, "Have care, son. Evil is afoot."

****

Energy gathered around her, like when Brigid would appear, making Evie glance about.

Another group from the tour came toward her. Their chatter was mind-numbing. A figure stirred behind them, tall with glowing blond hair. She blinked

25

as the man stepped to the side and then stopped. His brilliant white shirt and pants set him apart from the group as the people stepped into the light, passed her, and faded into the dark.

She lifted her camera to capture the apparition. The man in the frame smiled and posed. When she brought the lens to her eye, he winked. His hair shifted, and a pointed ear appeared. Within the camera lens, his face materialized in more detail. A memory flashed of Aodhán as she'd last seen him, as a youthful boy.

In the lens, the adolescent's face morphed into the man whose sharp jaw and royal nose hinted at the youth in the man before her. She clicked a few pics, but his image had her stopping.

When she lowered the camera, she checked the display, and she'd undoubtedly captured a shot of the man. In the photo, glowing white energy cast light from behind him, setting him in an eternal haze.

Her head shot up, and he stood before her. "Hello, Evie."

Her hand lifted as she moved it toward him, expecting it to pass through. When she touched his warm chest, she jerked back.

He captured it in his hand. "Aye, I'm real, Evie."

He brought her hand to his lips and brushed the back, kissing her. Tingles shot from her hand to her heart. Only one person affected her that way. *Aodhán.*

His grin grew as he lowered her hand. "I've been away, and for that, I am sorry. But I'm finally freed. Free to revisit the human realm."

Tears gathered in her eyes as he gazed into her eyes, her heart. Her Fae love, Aodhán, stood before her and held her hand.

"Evie, please let me make up my absence to ye. Let me show ye new hope and erase all doubt about yer feelings for me."

She whimpered as a tear fell. "Aodhán?"

His hand came up and caught her tear. He rotated his palm and held it open, presenting a clear gemstone shaped like a teardrop.

Handing it to her, he whispered, "I can only stay a moment, but tomorrow I shall come to ye. I'm glad ye kept the sphere. I heard yer call every time. No more tears, Evie."

He brushed a kiss on her lips. "Look for me tomorrow night in yer dreams. Don't lose hope."

Aodhán faded from her view.

Evie blinked. She turned around once, scanning the area. No one was about.

She turned again, calling out, "Hello?"

No one appeared on the street.

She pulled her camera up and pressed the button. Aodhán's smiling face and ethereal glow came into view. Proof he'd visited and she'd not seen a ghost.

Her fingers brushed her tingling lips at the promise of tomorrow night.

Chapter 3

Evie rolled over as the pounding beat inside her head. What a strange dream.

The front door slammed open as her da's voice carried through the flat, "Up, ye damn kids." He stomped through the apartment.

Kat's voice came softly to her, "Laird. Mac, I mean Laird MacDougall? What are ye doing here?"

Her da's gruff reply came after. "Good morn, or shall I say, 'good day' to ye, Kat."

Kat had taken to calling Evie's parents Laird and Mrs. Mac after the nickname Kat stuck with her. Something of an "in kind" gesture, Evie guessed.

Pots clanked. The loud sound of banging echoed through the flat. "Why ye all sleep till the nooning is beyond me. Up with ye kids. All of ye, up now!"

Doug's voice called out, "Ewan, yer da's here making a racket."

Her brother's voice beat a sharp reply, "Aye, I hear him. Shit, Da, all of Edinburgh hears ye."

Her da barked back, "Language, Ewan. Where's yer, sister?"

Evie rolled out of bed and shuffled into the common room, where everyone seemed to have assembled.

Her brother huffed, "Out late again, Evie?"

She eyed him full and well, knowing he'd only

returned from his time travel excursion with Doug an hour ago.

As she rubbed the sleep from her eyes, Evie turned to her da. "Dash, Da, why so early? Did ye drive up from Oban this morning? Ye were just here yesterday."

Laird Colin MacDougall glowered at them as he held a pot and pan, folding his arms. "Sit, all of ye."

Kat yawned and lay on the couch. Doug threw her legs off and sat in the space they'd occupied.

Ewan stood on the opposite side of the room from Evie, his "mind speak" coming to her, ~*Da's in a dander, what now?*~

Ever since the trip to Egypt, the mind-speaking power had grown stronger between the two. It worked flawlessly in the same room. They'd tested it over time, lengthening the distance. Shy of one kilometer, and it faded.

Evie shrugged and shuffled to the kitchen for some coffee. She picked up the kettle, filled it with water, plugged it in, and flipped the switch.

Her da called after her, "Ye can make me a cup as well!"

Evie groaned as she gathered cups for everyone—coffee for her and Da, tea for the rest.

The clatter of pots told her her da had set them down. "I must know, have ye kids encountered any Fae?"

Evie sucked in a breath as the kettle bubbled before her. Thank God she wasn't in the room. Her shocked expression would have been obvious. Still, she hid her face behind a cabinet as she pulled out tea and coffee. She tipped a measure of coffee grinds into the press as she yawned.

A mumble of no's filtered through the air. Evie sensed her brother had not replied, and she hadn't either.

She peeked around the corner as her da's sarcasm came through as he spoke. "Imagine my *surprise* and *dismay* when I woke this morning, went into my study, and the *Fae Fable Book* floated across the room, landing on my desk." He used his hands to mimic the floating book and waved both to the side as if presenting the book to them all.

The kettle whistled, making Evie jump. *The Fae Fable Book* only showed a story when the Fae needed a family member to search for a magic Fae Stone of Iona. She picked up the pot and poured hot water into each cup, then the coffee press. So far, her parents had recovered the Stone of Love, Kat and Doug's parents had located the Stone of Fear, and Auntie Ainslie had seen the Stone of Lust returned. Her uncle Dominic retrieved the most recent one, the Stone of Hope, eight years ago.

Evie placed tea bags in three cups and poured the coffee into the other two as she recalled that trip well. She and Ewan had accidentally got sucked back in time with Uncle Dom, and they found a stone in the Valley of the Kings, Egypt 1930s.

She carried three cups of tea, passing them to Doug and Kat.

Her da's sarcasm continued as she handed Ewan a cup. "The damn book fell open to the fable, the Stone of Doubt."

Her da grunted, eyeing each person in the room. "Damn it all, this time, the Fae let me read the whole damn tale!" The first time the book showed their father a fable, he'd only been allowed to read a portion at a time, as if to tease him with the information needed to find a magic Iona stone.

When her eyes met Ewan's, he shrugged as his "mind speak" came to her, *~Yer games or mine?~*

She stared as she replied, *~Yers for certain.~*

She moved back to the kitchen as her da continued his tirade, "It was some story about a bird captured by an evil warlock and kept from her true love who promised himself to a woman the warlock conjured, thwarting their love." He huffed, "The quote highlighted was, 'There is a sacredness in tears. They are not the mark of weakness but of power. The power of tears shall quell any person.' "

He nodded after reciting it. "Yer mother made me say it fifty times to ensure I repeated it correctly for ye."

She picked up the last cups and proceeded to her da, handing him one. "Thank ye, Evie." He sipped. "Ah, black. I needed it."

She knew, sensed it when he asked her to make a cup.

His eyes leveled in hers. "Ye see any Fae, Evie?"

She turned to sit in the chair, her eyes connecting with her brother's, who smirked.

She sipped her coffee, which was black as well, "No, Da."

Her da faced the rest of the room. "There was a second quote to this story. It was a long one. 'But let him ask in faith, with no doubting, for the one who doubts is like a wave of the sea that is driven and tossed by the wind.' "

Her brother shifted and sat opposite her. "Wait, Da.

Ye said the Stone of Doubt. That story's not about a bird but two kids exchanging marbles and candy. The boy kept one marble, and his doubt and obsession with greed kept him up all night, worrying the girl had kept back a piece of her candy."

Kat yawned. "The story of the bird sounds like that ballet we went to see with our moms, but that was about a swan."

When her da mentioned his version of the story, the ballet came to her mind as well, but Evie said nothing. Not yet. Not until she learned what or who the fable referred to—her, Ewan, Kat, or Doug. Clearly, her da felt it was one of the four. The Fae had already called upon each adult close to the family to search for a stone.

Her da blurted, "A ballet? Is that the one where the girl dies since her lost love made a vow to the wrong woman, and he battles the beast for her love, saving her life?" He groaned. "Bree kept me up night after night going on about lost love. I vowed never to let her see another classical ballet again."

The debate over the story continued around her as Evie sipped her coffee.

Her brother's gaze met hers, his eyebrow raised. *~A fable shown, but the wrong story for the Stone of Doubt. What does it mean?~*

Evie lowered her cup. *~It means ye have been time traveling again. 'Wave of the sea...' Was there a bird in yer pirate adventures, brother?~*

He snorted. *~ No, not a bird who's a woman. How about ye and yer ghosts?~*

His finger pointed at her. *~Where's yer Fae lover from Egypt? Aodhán. It's him this story is about.~*

Their da stepped between them. "Stop it, ye two! It's rude to talk when we can't hear yer minds." He slashed his hand to the side. "I hate it when ye do that near me. Sometimes I hear yer whispers, but nothing makes sense."

He stood between them, folding his arms across his massive chest. "Out with it, both of ye."

Ewan leaned around their da, grinning at Evie.

Evie answered her da's command, "The fable changed. The one ye read isn't the one Brigid had us read when we first learned all the stories." She shrugged. "This could be about anyone associated with the family, Da. Mrs. A, maybe the wharf lads." She let her voice trail off.

Ewan huffed, ~*Good one, sis, point the blame elsewhere.*~

She laughed aloud this time. ~*It's ye, I tell ye. How ye ever got the portal to go forward is beyond me.*~

Ewan grumbled, ~*Well, I figured part of it out, but time passes here when I'm gone.*~

Evie smirked. ~*Brigid said they'd forbidden going forward, yet ye break that rule as well as others daily. It's ye!*~

Ewan stood, stepping toward her, blurting, "It is not me. It's ye and yer Fae boy!"

Evie stood stamping her foot. "It's ye!"

Their da set his cup down and held his hands out, keeping the twins apart. "Whichever one it is, tell me so I know what we face."

Evie blinked and stared at her brother, her confidant in so much over the years as they learned and shared their growth in Fae powers.

She stepped back. "Da, I don't know if it's either.

That's the truth."

Ewan also moved back. "Aye, I don't know either."

Their da folded his arms. "Well, ye both keep an eye out and report back. The Fae called upon us, and it seems the Stone of Doubt needs finding."

Colin strode to the door, turned, and pointed at them. "Figure it out, but stay out of trouble. Call if ye need help. I love ye, but I've got to get back to yer ma. She's beside herself with worry, and I refused to allow her to come, fearful of what I'd find." He eyed the four in the room. "We love ye with all our hearts, but please be careful."

With a click and a slam, her da left the flat.

She whirled on her brother. "It's ye and yer pirate play! I know ye travel to the early eighteen hundreds with Doug, playing pirate almost nightly."

He strode to his room. "It's not playing." At the door, he turned, pointing a finger at her, looking very much like a younger version of their da. "It's a very profitable privateering business, and I'm *very* successful."

She laughed as she glanced at Doug, asleep on the couch.

Kat sat bug-eyed. "I always wanted to time travel."

Evie set her cup on the coffee table. "It's nothing really, but it gives ye a big headache."

Ewan called from his room, "It's ye and yer Fae boy."

Evie went to her room, slamming the door. What if it was her? After all these years, the Fae fable story appeared the morning after Aodhán. Was she the one set by the Fae to find the Stone of Doubt? And what was it with the change in story?

A tap came at her door. She knew it was Kat without opening it.

Kat spoke through the door, "What will ye do now?"

Evie said nothing. There was nothing to say. She didn't know what to do.

****

Evening came all too quickly as Evie stood before her mirror, analyzing her outfit. "Dress to impress," Manix's voice echoed. Evie eyed her reflection. All black. Black wide-leg slacks, black combat boots, and a baggy black blouse with a black tank underneath. Her black makeup accented the look with her kohl eyeliner and black blush. She wore blood-red lipstick, this time accentuating her full lips.

Dressy goth. Evie felt sexy as she puckered her lips. She turned, grabbed her small bag, and strode through the main living area. Kat sat watching the telly, some talk show with a purple and pink set, as her brother and Doug stood dressed in their eighteenth-century pirate garb. Both glanced up when she walked through the room.

Ewan whistled, "Wow, sis, no jeans? Must be a hot date."

She moved on, ignoring him as Kat giggled. "Manix asked her out. Told her to dress to impress."

Doug patted Ewan on the shoulder. "If that's dressing up, my shirt and trousers are perfect for a ball." He pulled his blade from his sheath, waving it in the air. "A ball on a pirate ship."

Evie stopped at the door. "Ewan, did ye ever stop to think Ma and Da can see when yer reproduction galleon ship disappears from Dunstaffnage Marina every night ye take it back in time?"

Doug slid his blade back into the holder as Ewan shrugged. "Not much different than yer ghosts?"

Evie barked a laugh. "A whole damn ship ye send back in time through the chapel door portal. However ye fit it, escapes me."

Ewan adjusted his cuffs. "Easy peasy. Gather yer energy into a swirling ball, open the portal, send the ball into the portal expanding the bend in time, and as ye move through, call yer ship to ye."

His eyes met hers. "Why ye never gathered energy and gave it to yer ghosts, making them whole so ye could capture a pic of a solid form, I don't understand."

Evie snapped at her bother, "Because sending energy to a ghost sends it wherever the soul must rest. Transitioning to heaven is beautiful, but hell…that's when I stopped helping them." A shiver passed over her, and she rubbed her arms. "Well, most."

Ewan crossed to her, rubbing her shoulder. "Sorry, sis, I forgot that part. So, a date with Manix, eh?"

She nodded, shaking off the chill. Ewan's hand stopped on her shoulder. *~The Fae boy? Giving up on him? I thought he was why the Fae story appeared.~*

Evie brushed his hand away. *~Not giving up; exploring my options. And the Fae story appeared because of ye.~*

She opened the door as her brother's reply rang in her head, *~Doubtful, but Evie, please be careful. Manix gives me dark vibes and casts doubt into my mind.~*

Her gaze met his, and she nodded before closing the door. Doubt—there it was again. Damn Fae fable had to be about Ewan.

****

Evie made a quick hike to the bar where she'd meet Manix. The restaurant combination bar was in an alleyway on the last part of The Long Mile, the road to Edinburgh Castle. Her regular ghosts appeared along the way from her flat to the castle, as the bar wasn't far from her employer, Maggie's Bar.

Nal, the toll booth gatekeeper, waved, but she didn't stop. Her feet beat a hasty step as she passed what was a bakery but was now a dress shop. The baker's ghost, Maureen, offered her a bun, but she waved her off. Spirit food wasn't something solid she could grab, let alone eat, but at times, she humored her ghostly friends, pretending to participate in their lives. Today, she didn't have the time.

Evie arrived at The Devil's Advocate Pub just as Manix walked out. "Evie, I came out looking for ye." His stare traveled over her body, making it seem like he caressed her where she stood.

He took her hand in his and kissed the back. "Black, my favorite color." It seemed it was. He wore a black suit that reflected an almost fluorescent glow when the light hit it. As he pulled her to his side and led them to a table, his dress shirt fell open, exposing his nearly bare chest, the muscles undulating as he moved.

When they arrived near the back of the restaurant, he stood before a table for two, set off from the rest. Evie sat at a table with a black tablecloth holding a formal setting, wine glasses, and a small candle. The setup gave Evie the impression of a perfect romantic dinner.

Manix passed her and sniffed deeply. "Yer scent. Vanilla with musk, but a heavier musk." As he turned his head, he breathed again. "Patchouli?" He huffed and breathed through his nose again as he whispered, "An intoxicating scent."

Manix sat opposite her and smiled.

A waiter appeared, opened a wine bottle, and offered Manix the cork to sniff.

Without taking his eyes off hers, Manix sniffed the cork and waved to the waiter to serve it. "I took the liberty of ordering the wine, merlot. A favorite of mine."

She'd had many wines at her family home. Her family often held formal dinners, since celebrating every milestone was a favorite of her ma's.

She took a sip. "Chardonnay is a favorite of my ma's, but I like the reds better."

Manix nodded as he sipped his. His nearly black eyes held hers as he set his glass down. The waiter appeared again, wordlessly handing them their menus. Evie glanced over hers, noting the chicken dish looked appealing.

The waiter returned and set down an appetizer platter of croquettes. Manix beamed as he served her one. "I ordered a starter, ham and brie croquettes."

Evie took the plate. "Thank you. Brie is a favorite of my ma's."

The waiter nodded as Manix addressed him. "The lady will have the chicken dish, and I the ribeye. No side, just the meat."

As the waiter took the menus, Evie spoke, "How…"

Manix's grin filled his face. "Hazarded a guess. I saw yer finger tap it as ye smiled."

He picked up his wine and sipped it as Evie took a

bite of the croquette. Flaky buttered pastry crunched as her teeth sank into the ham and cheese. The flavors burst over her mouth.

Manix picked up her wine and handed it to her. "Chase it with some wine. It enhances the cheese flavor." She took a sip, and he was right. The smoky red merlot enhanced the creamy snap of the cheese.

Ria, one of the girls from the wizard drama group, appeared with another man she recognized from a college drama production. Ria wore a linen crop top with a matching skirt that was so short if she bent over, everyone would see her full who-ha.

The girl strode confidently in four-inch platform spiked heels as the man with her fondled her rear. "Manix, slumming it tonight?"

The girl giggled, "Gothic ghost girl may be yer perfect match, Manix. All black."

Manix waved a hand without taking his gaze from Evie. "I will do as I wish. Off with ye, Carl and Ria." Both of his friends froze, and his eyes slowly slid to them.

Some unspoken signal must have occurred because Carl bowed. "My bad, Manix. She is as stunning as ye say."

They traveled away without further comment, and Manix took her hand in his. "Alone, at last." He fingered her hand. "I wish to spend this evening discussing my research into the spirit world. More importantly, the Fae realm."

Evie jolted but covered it, moving her hand from his and brushing her hair from her face.

Manix smiled. "But first, we eat."

The servers appeared with their plates and set each

before them. Hers held herb chicken in a creamed sauce and crispy haggis. His was a lone steak, the juices bleeding red over the plate. He cut into his and ate a large bite, humming as he chewed.

Evie cut into her chicken and sampled the small bite. It was quite good. They continued in silence, eating their dinner.

When Manix finished his lone steak, he took his wine glass and sat back in his chair. "I did much research for my play, for the warlock character. I spent the last months working on it, finding all I could on the Fae."

Evie set her fork down, nearly done with her meal but more nervous at Manix's direction of conversation. Friends had spoken of the Fae to her before, but mostly, it was playful references to the mysteries surrounding the mythical beings. Manix's tone carried something heavier and more sinister, giving her a chill that made her pause. He couldn't know of her powers, her connection to the Fae. Over the years, no one had figured it out. Even with her and Ewan's constant pranks, they'd come up with plausible explanations for each mysterious happening.

She picked up her wine glass. "Really? What did ye find?"

Manix's grin set her on edge. It appeared like her da's when he knew she lied.

His eyes stayed on hers as he spoke, "They have many magical powers. Some even stronger than the God almighty."

He pulled something from his pocket and held a stone in the light. Evie gasped before she caught herself. He held a marble stone, like a stone from the isle of Iona. She'd seen only one. Well, two halves of one, her parents' MacDougall love stone.

Her eyes met his as he stared at her over the stone. "I see ye recognize what type of stone this is, Evie. Aye, it's a stone from the isle of Iona. Rumored to possess magical properties."

He twirled it between his fingers. "Depending on who holds the stone, well, the powers within can strengthen." He fisted his hand around it. "I carried it as I worked on my play. It helped me realize the power of the warlock within." His eyes met hers. "The character that came to be inside me."

He opened his fist, and the stone lay in his hand. Before Evie knew what she'd done, her fingers grasped the stone, and energy flowed through her.

Manix wrapped his hand around hers. "I want ye to have it, Evie, please." He squeezed her hand. "I sense power within ye. Take the stone as a token of our friendship." He leaned forward and kissed her lips.

The waiter appeared, and Manix sat back, releasing her hand. "Dessert?"

Evie gripped the stone to her chest, and it warmed. She shook her head a little, overcome with emotion that a man gave her an Iona stone. A shared love stone like her parents had. No one had given her anything like it, and she wanted to cherish this moment. Did he know what he gave her, what it meant to her? Her memory flashed.

As a child, Evie took a stone half from Brigid, the MacDougall's Fae, and her mentor. "Wee bug. Listen well. Ye must give this to yer ma. The bad man took it from her and tossed it into the sea." Brigid held her hand, holding the stone. "This is the half of the

MacDougall love stone, one countless of loves pledged their devotion to one another over."

The memory flipped, and she sat with her ma in the Chapel in the Woods not long after she'd returned the stone.

"Evie, I never thanked you for returning my half of the love stone." Her ma held the stone, the sunlight flickering off the gem. "We made our wedding vows over the broken stones." Her ma held it to her heart. "I am so happy to have it back."

The memory faded as Manix stood and offered his hand to her. "I'll walk ye home, Evie."

She took it, pocketing her stone.

Manix spoke to the waiter as she rose, "Place it on my tab."

The server nodded as they strolled away, out of the bar, into the alley, and onto Market Street. The usually busy street was vacant this evening. Evie guessed it was later than she thought. A chilly breeze blew, and Manix's arm wrapped around her as they strolled down The Long Mile toward the college and her flat nearby. His body heated and warmed her as they continued down the street.

Neither spoke, and Evie seemed content.

The baker's ghost wasn't out when they passed what had been a bakery but was now a dress shop. At the toll booth, Nal, the gatekeeper, wasn't there either. Maybe it was much later.

Before Evie knew it, they stood at the door to her flat.

Manix took her hand on his. "I must work tomorrow, but there's an event in Edinburgh this weekend. Come with me on opening night, Friday?" He kissed her hand. "I'll enjoy taking ye. I'll pick ye up at nine after yer shift."

He bent to kiss her lips. Something flashed in her mind's eye. She backed up a bit. The image was difficult to make sense of.

She smiled and opened her door. "Aye, an event. I'd like that."

Manix nodded as Evie closed the door to him. She leaned against it. The image flashed in her mind again. A giant black glowing dragon flew above her. The roar echoed in her mind, as it had when Manix bent to kiss her. She fingered the Iona stone in her pocket and shivered.

****

Manix stood at her entryway as the door clicked closed. Her essence hovered in the air. Manix sniffed and picked up her scent again before it faded into the night. The deep musk called to him like no other. Could she be the one for him, his soul mate?

Her reaction to his gifting her the Iona stone was as he expected—touched and moved. He'd only collected the stone this morning, but the tale of his obsession with the warlock character was no lie. Finding the character living within him made him powerful. He detected it as he spent time with her.

Her scent and reactions. Her desire to seek the darkness of ghosts—it all fit. She was his and his alone. He turned and shifted into the shadows, finding comfort there.

Evie would bring him all he desired and more.

****

Exhaustion weighed on Evie as she closed the door to her flat. As she pushed away from the door, the events of the past days rolled over her mind, numbing it.

She went to her room and fell into the bed with her Iona stone held to her chest. Her lids grew heavy, and her hand released the stone.

She sensed sleep come upon her as a voice came to her in her haze. *~Evie, it's time.~*

She flinched, and her mind called back. *~Time for what?~*

Aodhán's voice came clearly to her. *~Time to visit my home, the Fae realm.~*

Chapter 4

The air hummed around Evie as the energy built. The buzzing in her ears told her a portal opened. Her world tilted and weaved like the last time she passed through a time gateway. She tried to wake but she couldn't as pressure pushed in on her from all around. A woman's scream echoed, and then all went silent.

Evie opened her eyes, and she stood in the clouds. She turned once, then again, and nothing appeared but clouds, yet she stood on something solid.

A hand touched her shoulder.

When she turned, she met Aodhán's smiling face. "Hello, Evie." His touch rooted her in the spot. The clouds blew away, revealing a room made of blue crystal that glittered in the dusk light. Aodhán rotated them as he kept his hands on her shoulders.

Before Evie was a large window the size of an entire room. They stood on a cliff, and beyond was a bright aqua sea that moved with soft waves as the sun set over the land, casting the sky in a warm tone of orange and red. A blue dragon flew overhead, flashing green in the sunlight as it screeched into the air as the beat of his wings came to Evie, steady with each whoosh.

She breathed as Aodhán wrapped his arms around her, pulling her against his muscular chest. "Welcome to Broemere Castle, my home."

She turned as he held her in his arms. "Yer home? Ye mean the Fae realm?"

Aodhán brushed his fingers over her cheek. "Aye." He gazed at her momentarily with a grin spread over his face. "Come, I wish to show ye around the castle before we meet the others."

He pulled her hand, and she tugged back, stopping him. "The ball, it still calls ye?"

He nodded as he turned, and she tugged again. "Ye mentioned punishment. What for?"

He took her hand and kissed the back. "For showing ye spells I wasn't allowed to."

Evie stood staring at him as the edges of his eyes crinkled. She looked down, her mind rolling over memories as the past connected with the present, then his statement.

She gasped. "The Fae, they punished ye for helping me." Her eyes connected with his. "Yer punishment was because of me. Ye didn't leave me. They kept ye away."

Aodhán stepped to her, his hand on her cheek. "Aye, that's true." He bent and brushed a kiss. Tingles like before shot to her toes, electrifying her body.

Aodhán's whisper brushed her ear. "And I'd do it all over again." He stepped back. "But now a tour."

He took her hand and placed it on his arm as he strode across the vast room. "This is the throne room." He pointed to two chairs on a dais, much like she'd seen in her ma's history books. When they walked past, Aodhán chuckled. "My grandda rules with an iron fist and a soft heart." He hummed. "As I will one day."

They exited the room and entered a busy hallway. People traveled at a brisk pace, some coming, some going. The men wore the identical soft fabric suits Aodhán wore but in different hues of pastels. The woman all donned flowing fabric dresses that looked straight from Greek times, each of differing style and length, also soft pastel hues. Not one stopped to give them notice.

Evie shifted behind Aodhán, hiding her all-black garments, feeling out of place.

Aodhán patted her hand, and a woman appeared. "Evie, please follow me."

Evie glanced back at him, and he nodded. "Erna will bring ye to me when ye finish." He kissed her hand before releasing it. "In my kingdom, Evie, fear not. Ye are safe."

Erna led her down a hall as Evie glanced at Aodhán over her shoulder. He smiled and waved. When Erna stopped before a door, the door faded, disappearing like a space movie.

As they stepped inside, Evie's eyes traveled over the room. The floor, walls, and ceiling had white and blue patterned tile, much like old Greek photos from her ma's history books. A square sunken tub sat on the floor with fragrant water that filled the room with steam. Sweet gardenias filled the air, reminding Evie of summers at Dunstaffnage.

Erna took her hand. "As Aodhán told ye, I'm Erna, a servant to the royal family. My instructions are to bathe and dress ye for the formal meeting with the King of the Fae." She flicked her wrist, and Evie's clothing faded as a soft, fluffy robe wrapped around her. Evie bent, and even her boots vanished.

Erna giggled. "Ye are human. Getting used to our ways will take time, but most humans like them." She waved to the tub. "There's soap for yer body and special wash for yer hair." There was a pause, and then she spoke again from farther away, "When ye finish, I'll be back."

Evie glanced over the bath, finding the items Erna indicated. When she turned to thank her, the Fae was gone. Left alone, Evie did the only thing left to do. Get into the tub.

When she did, the water was a bit warm, and she sighed. A wave went through the water, which cooled to a temperature she liked. She made quick work of her wash, including her hair. She scrubbed the red lipstick and black makeup off.

When she felt she'd finished, she took one step from the tub, and Erna appeared with a thick towel. "Here, Mi'lady."

Evie jolted but stepped into the wrap, appreciating its warmth. When she turned around, her hair had dried, and she wore a gown like the women in the hall. Hers was of fine silk with gold thread running through it, falling full length to the floor. As she shifted, the fabric caressed her naked body beneath, making her feel sensual and sexy. When she turned again, her toes peeked out, and soft sandals covered them.

Evie turned before a mirror, examining her reflection. Her hair hung in her natural dark brown waves past her shoulder, soft and shining. Her face glowed nearly pink, and her lips looked a little peach. Her blush rose as she noted how glamorous and mature she looked.

She turned to Erna. "How?"

"Ye'll get used to our ways soon." Erna bowed and waved. "Follow me, please."

The servant led her out of the room into a vacant hall. As they rounded the corner, the gown flowed easily with Evie's step. She'd not worn a full-length dress, but this one felt nice, dressy but natural. They approached another corner and passed another large window overlooking the same brilliant ocean.

At the door, Erna paused. The door faded just like the last had.

When they cleared the entryway, a booming voice echoed, "She's finally here? I am so happy!" A large man in a glowing white suit came to her. His arms opened wide as he took her into a giant hug. Warmth and safety flowed over her, and a sense of ease washed through her.

When he pulled back, he kissed her on the cheek. "Welcome, Evie." His breath held the faint scent of whisky, like when her da had a dram.

Aodhán's voice came to her. "Grandda. Ye scare her."

The large man stepped back, and Aodhán came beside her. "Evie, my grandda, Dadga…"

As her regard returned to the man, she finished the sentence, "The king of the Good Fae, the Tuatha Dé Danann." Her eyes went between the men, and she quickly saw the resemblance as another fact clicked into her head.

Her head shot up. "If ye are Dagda, then Brigid is yer daughter."

Aodhán's smile grew as he turned her, and Brigid stood beside a window similar to the one in the hall. "Hello, wee bug."

Evie yelped and ran into her mentor's welcoming arms, "Brigid, I haven't seen ye in so long."

They rocked side to side as Brigid held her tighter. "Ye grew up. Needed me less and less as yer powers grew."

Evie stepped back, releasing her mentor's arms, and her eyes stayed on Brigid. "Aodhán is yer son." Her head turned to Aodhán. "The story ye told all those years ago. The Fae boy with the powers. It was ye."

Aodhán nodded.

Evie glanced between the three in the room. "The *Fae Fable Book*. It changed. Is this why I'm here?" The three in the room exchanged glances as they grew quiet.

Evie paced, recalling all she could from her father's short visit to the flat. "Da mentioned two quotes. The first, 'There is a sacredness in tears. They are not the mark of weakness but of power. The power of tears shall quell any person.' "

She stopped, staring at the floor, trying to recall the second. When it came to her, she exclaimed, " 'But let him ask in faith, with no doubting, for the one who doubts is like a wave of the sea that is driven and tossed by the wind. No doubts, only my love and I will prevail.' "

Aodhán stepped forward and took her hands in his. "The book changes when it wants. Most times, we can't control it."

His eyes moved between his relatives, then settled back on her. "I can't tell if the story speaks of ye or Ewan. The future is hard to see since the evil Fae created the three evil stones that hunt the good stones."

Evie glanced down. "But the story changed…"

Dagda waved his hand as a servant brought drinks in for them all. "Tonight isn't about business, but pleasure. We welcome a newcomer to the Fae realm and celebrate yer reunion!"

A tall older brunette came in through a fading door, followed by another younger person of her likeness.

Dagda's voice boomed again, "Ah, my wife and love. Tethra and my other daughter…"

Evie grinned as both women approached. "Morrigan!" She first hugged Tethra, who smelled of roses like her ma, and then Morrigan, whose scent was lilies like Marie, Kat, and Doug's mom.

When she turned, Aodhán handed her a glass, thick but light-weight and filled with a glowing blue liquid.

He leaned in, whispering, "We call this the Heart of the Fae, much as yer family calls its whisky the Heart of Scotland."

She started to take a sip, but Aodhán's hand stalled her. "Careful, Evie. It's very potent on humans."

Dagda's voice boomed again, "A toast to Evie and the Fae!"

Everyone took a sip, and Evie bent, taking a small sip. The smooth drink passed her lips, then her tongue, and raspberry lemon whisky tarted her mouth—a favored drink of hers. She tilted the glass up, expecting to find the rich pink liquid she tasted, but the blue glowing liquid swished in the glass.

Aodhán chuckled beside her. "It's a charm. Ye taste yer favored drink, no matter what we put inside."

Evie thought of another drink, wanting to test the taste spell. She filled her mind with another whisky drink, one of a plain shot of her family's label, the Heart of Scotland. When she took a larger sip, the shock of pure whisky passed directly into her throat, causing her to cough.

Everyone in the room laughed.

As Aodhán took the glass from her, he said, "Every human has the same reaction. They test the theory behind the spell."

He set the glass down away from Evie. "And now ye know why it's so potent on humans. Ye are unable to resist it."

Aodhán turned to his grandda, Dagda. "If I may, I'd like to show Evie the Moon Garden before her visit ends."

Evie turned to him. "Over? I just got here!"

Dagda waved them on. "On with ye kids."

Aodhán led her to the door, and when it faded open, Dagda called, "Aodhán, ye kids keep to the rules now. Her visits have a time limit for her safety."

Aodhán took her hand in his, and they proceeded through the door.

When it faded shut, Evie tapped Aodhán's arm. "My safety? What does he mean?"

Aodhán kissed her cheek. "I have to have ye back in the human realm before sunrise, or ye'll turn into a pumpkin."

Aodhán flicked his wrist, and the castle faded as a lake with a waterfall bathed in silver moonlight appeared before them. Evie glanced around and noted they stood on a boulder overlooking the lake.

She gasped. "It's dark already?"

Aodhán took her in his arms. "Time bends here. To ye, it's an unnatural passing. It's one of the reasons ye must time yer visits."

A rustling came from behind her. As she turned, a white unicorn burst from the brush. The animal stood still and stared at Evie.

Her breath caught as Aodhán's arms tightened

around her. "Don't move. 'Tis rare that one appears, and before ye like this, it's magical."

The stallion dipped his head as he approached them. Evie took a deep breath as Aodhán's arms loosened. As the stallion inched closer, Evie's desire to reach out to touch the creature overcame her. She raised her hand, and the stallion nuzzled it. The soft, fuzzy touch tickled, making Evie smile.

Aodhán gasped. "Never have I seen one approach a Fae, let alone a human. They are revered animals with their own magic."

Evie brushed his nose again, and the creature blew once, then nibbled her hand.

Aodhán took a deep breath and then whispered in her ear, "My grandda described them as beasts able to outrun humans and other animals, which is impossible for a human to capture unless encircled by an army of men and horses. Even Fae powers are of no use to this rare creature." The stallion dipped his head, then raised it, nudging her hand again as if craving her touch.

"The animal would rather fight—with its horn, teeth, and hooves—and die free than live as a captive. It's why they preside as Scotland's national animal, symbolic of the country's stubborn bravery."

She felt Aodhán grin as he spoke. "He described the creature as ye see before ye now. A white-bodied equine mystic, tamed only by a virgin's hands. Many claim the horn purifies water and cures disease."

Her gaze traveled the creature's features. The horn jutting from the forehead twisted like a corkscrew made of the color cream, spun with a silver luminescent streak—like the inside of an oyster shell.

Aodhán squeezed her once as he huffed, "It's

claimed unicorns nestled in the Virgin Mary's lap—a symbol of purity and benevolence. Grandda said only a being of pure heart can draw a unicorn to them like ye have today."

Evie whispered, "I am of pure heart?"

Aodhán's breath tickled her ear as he breathed back, "Aye, always have been and always will be. It's one of the things that's drawn me to ye."

His voice held wonder, making the moment much more special. "Evie, yer own unicorn."

Evie brushed the stallion's cheek as a sense of belonging and purpose washed over her. The animal lifted his head, tossed it once, turned, and took off into the woods.

Aodhán turned her to him and caressed her cheek. "The unicorn stands for our desire for others to see us as extraordinary. The animal's lore allows humans and Fae to believe that we, too, are special—if only we were allowed to live unconstrained and if we didn't have to conform ourselves to fit into the world around us. They are the ultimate rare being—a wild spirit we discern in ourselves, one that can bring destruction and relief, violence and healing."

He took both her hands in his and then glanced away. "So much is the same in the Fae realm as the human. Given our rising sea levels, ongoing wars, and the ambient uncertainty of the now, we're ever more aware of how precarious the realms really are. Yet we continue to survive, even as the structures we've created crumble before our eyes, leaving us alone as we always were, in the woods."

Her eyes returned to the trees where the unicorn fled, alone in the woods, yet not alone.

Aodhán's hand came to her cheek. "Ye are special, Evie. To have a unicorn come to ye."

She turned to him as he hummed, "My sweet Evie, I should have known a unicorn would come to ye. Ye have bewitched me all this time."

He bent and kissed her, brushing his lips against hers.

She leaned into him, rising on her toes to kiss him back.

He chuckled and pulled back. "Evie, ye tempt me beyond reason. Even those human years ago, as teenagers."

He bent and brushed his lips against hers again, whispering into the kiss, "I plan to visit ye often, Evie MacDougall." He kissed her, and at her sigh, he thrust his tongue against hers, twirling it in a maddening dance that left her breathless. "I have so much time to make up for and too little time to make it happen." Evie relished his craving, his touch, his caresses.

His hands drifted to her shoulder, and the gown floated to her feet. Aodhán stepped back as his eyes roamed her body. He came to her, kissing her deeply as he took her into his arms again. He shifted, picked her up, and lay on the cliff's ledge. Her back rested on a pillow of soft leaves and moss.

Aodhán's hand came to her beast and cupped it, sending tingles through her. She ran her hands over his chest and slid into the collar of his shirt. He sat up and ripped the shirt off as buttons flew.

Evie giggled. "A Fae, and he must rip his shirt off instead of making it fade from view."

Aodhán covered her with his body. "Clothing fading from view. Is that a request?"

Evie's mind conjured the vision, and Aodhán's grin widened as his naked body brushed against hers. Heat flashed over her as she relished the feeling of his hard body against hers. His hand returned to her breast, and his mouth followed as he suckled her nipple. Evie gasped, and her hands gripped his shoulders while his mouth worked magic on her. First one, then the other—her breasts never tingled like this before. Sensation woke in her body as Aodhán's hand trailed down her stomach, his fingers leaving a trail of fire. When his fingers brushed her, she jerked a little.

His head came up, and he kissed her lightly, "Is it okay that I touch ye, there?"

Evie's hand trailed down his chest over his rippled belly and gripped him. He sucked in as his head dropped back. "By the gods, woman, do ye know what that does to a man?"

Evie kissed him, speaking between the thrusts of her tongue, "To a man, aye, to a Fae, not yet."

His hand nudged on her, his fingers parting her as they rubbed her.

She moved her hand over him, up then down to the base, her fingers tickling the sacs below.

Aodhán growled as his head came up, and their eyes met. "Evie…"

She kissed him as her hand wrapped around him, moving over him. He returned the kiss and slid a finger inside her. Her hand over him, his finger on her, they kept a rhythm matching their kisses as each built in intensity. Soon, both panted as the energy inside Evie climbed to a height, she knew not what.

Aodhán threw his head back, crying out her name. Evie closed her eyes as his hand went faster. Soon, she felt the wall of energy inside her burst, stars flashed behind her lids, and warmth covered her hand.

Aodhán gathered her in his arms as his hand waved over them, his magic cleansing their bodies, their clothing fading onto them. Evie pouted, wanting to stay and lie with him, naked as they had before. When she blinked, they stood at the cliff again.

Aodhán held her tightly. "Yer time is almost up."

His grip on her tightened. "What I wouldn't give to keep ye here, to spend eternity with ye."

Evie whimpered, "Then do so."

Aodhán lifted his head and kissed her nose. "Oh, Evie. I wish it could be that simple. But it's not. I've seen yer fate. It's not here in the Fae realm."

She rose on her toes again, kissing his mouth as he held her tight, returning her kiss, tasting her as he had before.

Her head swam, and all she wanted was him. "Please, Aodhán. Make the darkness go away. Show me only this light."

He stepped back, holding her hand. "If ye stay Evie, ye can never return to the human realm. Ye are not immortal." He kissed her hand. "I promise to visit again. Tomorrow night, look for me in yer dreams. Ye have the ball of energy and now the tear gem. They call me if ye need me."

He let go, and she floated, drifting in her dream.

*****

The sun shone brightly on her face. Evie rolled over to avoid the brightness. Her right hand gripped something sharp, and she slowly opened her eyes as she opened her hand. Inside sat the clear white teardrop gem Aodhán made from her tear. She sat up, flipping her long hair aside, and held the gemstone to her heart. He said it called him.

She shifted, and the silken fabric of her dress brushed her naked body beneath, like in the Fae realm. Evie glanced about her room, and folded neatly on her chair before her desk sat her black clothing from the night before. Her black boots were on the floor beside the chair, shining clean.

So, her visit to the Fae realm was no dream. She rolled to the side of her bed, and a rock cut into her hip. She shifted aside, and Manix's Iona stone lay on the bed. She picked it up and held each stone to the morning's sunlight. They both flashed. Manix's stone burned hot. She dropped it, gasping at the intense heat. Evie rubbed her hand, letting the sting fade. She looked at the Iona stone on the floor, which appeared normal. She picked it up and placed both side by side on her dresser.

When her head came up, she caught her reflection in the mirror and admired her new look. Chestnut brown, long, flowing hair cascaded down her shoulder. The silken gown flowed over her curves when she stood, accentuating them sensuously. She grinned. Well, nothing felt normal, but all new—a new day and a new Evie.

****

Aodhán faded into the Fae realm to the room he'd left only moments ago to first visit Evie. Brigid, his mother, stood there with a knowing look in her eye.

Aodhán strode to the decanter filled with Heart of the Fae, filled a glass, and swallowed it all.

His mother laughed. "After so long, I would think seeing yer true love would ease yer tension, not raise

58

it."

Aodhán set the glass down. "I have so much to catch up on. So much to make up for." He strode to the window overlooking the ocean. "How do I do it? If I give her all my heart at once, I may scare her basic human sensibilities. She's had much time without me, without us."

Brigid came to him, patting his shoulder. "My son, ye will figure it out. But take care." She released him and stepped back. "Ye still have yer duties here in the Fae realm. Yer destiny lies here. Evie's is in the human realm. Ye know this."

Aodhán took a deep breath. It was a confusing mess. The fate of Evie, he easily saw, was a love marriage with a child and happiness in the human realm—her love's identity, blocked from his view.

The Fae prophesied his fate thousands of years ago. The grandson born with the greatest Fae powers of all would take his place as king over the Tuatha Dé Danann and oust the latest and most evil ruler of the Fomoire Fae, their new king.

It couldn't be so, but fate showed him the outcome, much like *The Fae Fable Book* showed the fate of the person finding a Stone of Iona.

His true love, found in Evie—yet their ends were not together. Each of them existed in a different realm, serving a different purpose for the good of all.

Yet, Colin MacDougall, Evie's da, had changed the outcome of a fable. Could he change the outcome of destiny?

He turned to his mother, who shook her head. "Changing the outcome of one's destiny, son, comes at a great cost." She sighed. "And I suspect the powers will not permit ye to see the different outcomes of each choice." She leveled her eyes on his, much as she had in his youth, "Tempting fate, tempting the rath of destiny. Son, ye play with powers greater than even ye."

Aodhán fisted his hands. "I will find a way. Evie and I are true loves. I have no doubt true love will conquer all. I only need to find a way."

Chapter 5

Evie threw open Kat's door, allowing it to bang against the wall.

Kat rolled over. "Kind of early, even for ye, Evie."

Evie strode to Kat's closet, flipping through each item. She didn't say a word, fearful she'd give away something, anything that told her best friend she'd visited the Fae realm.

Kat sat up. "What are ye wearing? Yer hair's lighter. I like it!"

Evie glanced down, forgetting the Fae gown, and shrugged. "Something for a play." She cringed inside at lying to her friend but couldn't tell anyone she was the one the Fae fable referred to. Not yet, at least.

Evie flipped back and forth between a crop top and a skirt. Kat's chest was like her ma's, larger than Evie's, but Evie's hips were bigger. Her clothes had to fit. Evie didn't have time to go shopping. She wasn't ready for the idea of selecting new clothing that she'd never bothered to glance at, let alone try on.

Grabbing the pink crop top and gray pencil skirt, Evie felt comfortable with it being long enough to cover her knees. She had to start somewhere. If she wore a miniskirt to work, ha! Evie envisioned falling, carrying ale, and flashing her personals to all of Maggie's Bar. That'd be a hoot.

As Kat called after her, she strode from the room.

"Sure, ye can borrow some of my clothes. Thanks for asking!"

In her room, Evie stripped the Fae gown and hung it, carefully placing it in the back of her closet. She slipped on a bra and undies and donned the crop top, lifting her arms to ensure her boobs stayed covered. With the skirt on, she examined herself in the mirror.

"Nice. Not yer usual colors." Kat leaned on the mirror frame, yawning. "The form-fitting cotton looks good."

Evie turned right, then left, checking her reflection. It needed something more. She moved to her closet, examining her belts. The skinny suspenders, that's what it needed. Attaching those, she turned before the mirror and nodded.

As she sat to put on her black boots, Kat collapsed on her bed. "Why the change?" She rolled over. "Not that I'm complaining, but pink with light gray and form-fitting cotton isn't yer norm."

Kat sat up. "Manix! It has to be. Ye have the hots for Manix!"

Evie shrugged as she brushed her long hair out. This was good. If they thought she spent her time with Manix, they wouldn't figure out she'd spent most of the evening in the Fae realm with Aodhán.

She placed her hair in pigtails and began braiding each one. She had to keep her hair up for her waitressing, but after work, when she went out with Manix, the braids would make her hair wavy when she let it out. Perfect.

Speaking of Fae realms, "Where's Ewan and Doug?"

Kat stood and went to the door. "In bed as usual.

They come back later and later each trip." She sighed. "They should be careful."

Evie checked the clock. *Dash, it's almost eleven am*. Her shift started at noon, and Manix said he'd pick her up at nine when her shift ended.

She grabbed her leather jacket and went past Kat, who held her arm. "Do ye know what ye are doing with Manix? Ewan mentioned that some say he has a temper he can't control."

Evie pulled her arm away. "It's nothing. I'm sure exaggeration."

Evie ran to the door as Kat called after her, "Sure, don't mind me, yer *BFF*. I *only just* arrived, and ye are off every evening with a man." She sighed dramatically. "I'll stay in with a movie *again*."

Evie stopped at the opened door. "Soon, ye and I will go bar hopping. Introduce ye around."

Kat chuckled, "Hold ye to it."

Evie wasn't certain what this day held. She'd not dated many men, as none seemed to appeal to her. Ewan said it was because she compared them all to her Fae boy, and maybe she had. A human could never beat out the attraction a Fae held. It wasn't a mere myth, but the total truth.

Dressed and ready, Evie turned to go out her bedroom door. The gemstones flashed on her desk. She flung her hand out as she gathered power, pulling the Iona stone to her. The stone Manix gave her flew into her hand. She pocketed it as she moved through the flat and out the front door onto the street.

Evie turned to The Long Mile, Market Street, to make her way to work. Saturday morning had dawned into a sunny, warm day, but she kept her coat on. The crop top left her midriff bare, a feeling she'd have to grow used to.

When she passed the toll booth, Nal, the ghost, called out, "Evie, ye look lovely today. Why, a skirt like a proper woman." Evie waved but didn't call back. Other people crowded the street. Calling to a person only she could see, well, it just wasn't something to do.

When she passed the dress shop, the baker's ghost, Maureen, was out handing out hot buns. With the area empty of people, Evie stopped and pretended to sample her wares.

Maureen nodded. "Fine day it is, and ye look fancy today."

Evie brushed her pretend crumbs off and smiled. "Thanks, Maureen. Have a good day."

She entered the Garden District and the area before Maggie's Pub. Evie glanced about, searching for her ghost friend but not finding her. She was early for her shift and wanted to speak to her Maggie. Evie sat on a bench and waited, hoping the apparition would appear. She had a question for her.

Evie sat for a while, watching tourists come and go. Some hiked up Victoria's Street, marveling at the brightly colored shops. Another group stopped to examine the plaque with the names of those hung over the years at Grass Market Square.

A shadow traveled over her from behind, blocking the sun as a breath blew near her ear.

A heady musk scent came to her. "Ye look lovely in the sunlight. But the dark truly accentuates yer beauty." She turned, and Manix sat on the bench behind her, their heads bent close. So close when she turned, their breaths mingled. Her hand went to the Iona stone in her pocket. The one he'd given her, and it warmed in her hand.

Manix's jet-black hair and dark eyes seemed to absorb the sunlight. His back robes for his tours as a student from that wizard movie added to his dark vibe.

He sniffed and rocked back as a frown crossed his face, "Gardenias? Last night, yer scent was musk, heavy and alluring. And yer hair is lighter."

Evie brushed her neck, forgetting about the Fae bath. Was her scent really that obvious?

Manix brushed her face with his fingers, and they stopped while gripping her chin. "The patchouli I like. Ye will wear it tonight." His gaze held hers, the black in his eyes flashing. He bent and kissed her full, his tongue thrusting in, taking her unaware. She responded, unsure if she liked his forcefulness but craved his attention. His words echoed in her head—*the patchouli, wear it.*

He sucked her lip as he pulled back. "Till this evening. In the meantime, my graveyard calls." He stood gracefully as his robes flared.

He strode down the street, calling out to the tourists gathered along The Long Mile, "Come one, come all to the wonderful world of wizards. A tour not for the faint of heart in the Friar's Kirkyard." His voice faded as he rounded the corner, and Evie marveled at his overwhelming presence.

Maggie's voice startled her. "Ye wanted to ask about that one. I waited and watched. Black as night, sinful as the devil, and pure evil follows the man." Maggie gave the crow's feet sign with her hand, an old sign to ward off the devil.

The ghost spoke in a haunting tone, "Something

65

lives inside him, something dark and dangerous."

Evie brushed it off with a laugh. "Aye, I suppose ye say that of all men. Something always lurks inside them. It's called hormones."

Evie went to rise as Maggie grabbed her arm, gripping her in a way a ghost usually couldn't. "I meant what I said, Evie. Be careful."

Evie nodded and stood staring at the corner Manix had just turned. "Aye, women are to be wary of all men. It's the way it's always been."

When she turned back, Maggie wasn't there. Evie turned around, glancing around her, and found only tourists.

Her boss, Hal, called from the bar entrance, "Evie, yer shift's begun!"

****

Nearly done in after a long afternoon and night on her feet, Evie shoved her way into the women's restroom. Her date with Manix approached. In the bathroom, she sniffed herself, and the scent of ale, grease, and sweat greeted her—what she wouldn't give for a bath, even a human one. But Manix was to meet her. She dug in her purse, thankful her perfume bottle was at the bottom. Evie uncorked it, and the heavy musk scent filled her nostrils. Patchouli. She dabbed some on her neck and wrists, undid her braids, and ran her fingers through her long, wavy hair. Evie grabbed her makeup bag and pulled out the lipstick, avoiding the black eyeliner and powder. Using her finger, she dotted some on her cheeks and rubbed it in as a blush. She smeared some on her lips, leaving a tint of red, but not the blood red the color truly was.

Evie stopped and examined her reflection. Did she

look any different, having traveled to the Fae realm? She felt changed, like something had blossomed inside her, growing from a bud to a flower, petal by petal. She stared in wonderment. Only yesterday, a girl stared back, one with pigtails and black makeup, trying to be a woman. Today, a woman stared back, with long, lighter hair loose, a blush on her cheeks, and a determination in her expression. She nodded once. There was no going back, only forward.

She grabbed her stuff and shoved it in the bag as she pushed her way out the door of the women's restroom.

She strode to the door as Hal called out, "Have a nice time!" Evie waved and exited the door and entered the street. Crowds gathered on the corner as a group pushed past her into the bar. She sidestepped, wondering where Manix was.

When she turned back, he stood before her, "Ye're late. What kept ye?"

Evie grinned, "I had to freshen up." She flipped her hair, hoping he liked it loose.

Manix huffed, "I don't like it when people are late."

Evie shrugged and turned, tossing her hair again. "Well, I can always go home."

Manix grabbed her arm and brought her flush against his body. His nose came close to her ear as he buried it in her long hair.

He took a deep breath through his nose and let it out as his arms moved around her, circling in his embrace. "Yer scent, is that why ye are late?" He sniffed again and let it out in one long groan.

Evie could only manage a nod.

Manix growled as he kissed her ear. "Ye obeyed my command."

He pulled back, a scowl on his face. "Don't be late again."

He took her hand and strode down Market Street, then down The Long Mile away from Edinburgh Castle. He wore all black again, although it was jeans, a tee, and a leather jacket this time. Evie carried hers. The warmth from the bar still lingered.

Manix kept a quick pace as Evie had to skip to keep up.

Evie tugged on his hand as they turned left on South Bridge and headed up Princes Street. "Manix, I am near running. Can we slow down a bit?"

Manix stopped. His glare was one she couldn't read. She heaved as they stood there, but she was grateful for the rest.

Manix pushed to her and kissed her full on the lips. "Come, I take ye to something I am truly proud of." He walked down the street at a more measured pace. "For years, I've worked with this group to bring the arts to Edinburgh, to all of Scotland."

Evie's head came up, and they headed to Calton Hill, where a large group assembled. As they came closer, music and a crowd filled the air.

She glanced at Manix. "Is this The Hidden Door Project?" She sighed. "I've always wanted to come but could never get tickets."

Manix smiled as he brought two tags on lanyards out from his jacket pocket. "Ye will have tickets, Evie. An all-event pass to everything, including behind the scenes."

Evie stopped as Manix placed the lanyard over her

head. He beamed as he placed his on.

Carl stumbled into them, nearly knocking Evie over. "Manix, ye finally made it!" He had Ria in tow in a short dress and high heels.

Carl nodded to Evie. "Evie. A delight."

At his gracious greeting, her mouth fell open. Only yesterday, he'd made fun of her, calling her "gothic girl."

Carl fell in step with them, Ria on his arm as he chatted. "Evie, welcome to The Hidden Door Project. We open up forgotten urban spaces for the public to explore and discover incredible music, art, theatre, film, dance, spoken word, and more." The first performing group they came upon performed in a tent beside the road. Singers with a four-person string quartet played Renaissance music. Evie tried to stop, but Manix pulled her along.

They shifted to the side of the road, passing other fairgoers as Carl kept his commentary going, "Through our festivals, we reveal hidden parts of Edinburgh to showcase new and emerging artists, musicians, theatre, and filmmakers. The festival had steadily grown in size and reputation since 2014, when we cleared out the abandoned Market Street vaults to run a nine-day arts festival focused on showcasing local creative talent. From our clearing, people now can visit the vaults at night." They passed a couple of food vendors as the smell of baked cinnamon bread wafted to Evie. The next stall held jugglers who were street performers Evie recognized from frequent summer performances in Grass Market.

Manix kept in step with Carl while keeping a firm grip on Evie's arm. Ria trailed behind, addressing Evie.

"I like yer outfit. This year's festival will be one for the books."

Carl turned the corner, and three large stages came into view. "We've brought to life places like the hidden courtyard behind Kings' Stables Road and the old Leith Theatre that started transforming the building into the major arts venue the city needed."

Ria giggled. "I performed at the old Leith Theatre last year."

Carl led them into the main school building, and within the entry was a lobby, and beyond a complete stage, which seemed ready for a show.

Carl stopped. "Last year, we transformed the derelict former State Cinema building, the epic Granton Gasworks in north Edinburgh." He glanced back and waved his hand before them. "Thanks to a healthy donation from a wealthy contributor, we have brought the old Royal High School on Calton Hill to life this year. The building has been mostly silent since the school closed in the 1960s. After we finish, work transforms it into Scotland's new National Centre for Music."

Evie stared all around her, wondering who the generous soul was who gave so much.

Carl bowed to Manix, "Thank ye again, Manix, for yer generous donation." He smirked. "I'll leave ye both to it."

As they strolled away, Ria called over her shoulder, "Evie, love yer hair." They both turned, and the crowd swallowed them.

Evie turned to Manix, his stare intent as she spoke. "Ye? I thought ye worked yer way through school. Yer the donor?"

Manix brushed her hair from her face. "There is much about me, Evie, ye don't know. My family has a long and interesting history. While I am the only one left, money is something I do have."

Evie folded her arms. "But ye work almost daily for the tour group."

Manix grinned. "Aye, but I work for myself. The tour is a favorite of mine. The graveyard, a place I find solace."

He took her hand and placed it on his arm. "Come, we will watch the show from the wings."

Manix led them around, and the curtains hung as wings, making the temporary theater space. Many waved to him as he positioned them out of the way, yet in full view of the play. The lights dimmed, and the large room went pitch back. Manix stood behind Evie, holding her in his arms.

His breath brushed her ear as he spoke lowly, "This is another of my creations. An extension to the warlock's story. They'll act it out in mime, so I'll narrate for yer enjoyment." He kissed her ear, and she hummed, leaning against him.

The stage lights came up, and a lone woman dressed as a princess stood on the stage. Her long black hair hung much like Evie's had before.

She sensed Manix's smile in his voice. "A princess pure and innocent." A man with a unicorn head entered the stage and galloped around her, tossing his fake head. He stopped and kneeled, then lay on the ground, seeming injured.

Manix's voice spoke soft yet firm, "A princess comes across a unicorn injured in the woods." The princess knelt beside the man and rubbed her hands down his leg. She sat beside him and held his head in her lap, caressing the head like a lover.

Manix's lips brushed her ear. "She heals him, and he is forever grateful." Manix shifted, and his entire body came against her back. His arousal was evident as he rubbed against her. Sensations flooded her as his hands roamed her body. She flushed hot, then cold. The images of a man and woman together naked in bed flashed in her mind's eye.

Manix brushed her hair aside, and his tongue trailed her ear. "The unicorn laid his head on her lap as he gripped her hard. The wind swirled around them as the forest grew dark."

The wind sound filled the room as the lights dimmed to near blackness. Manix rubbed himself against her as his hand found her breast, and he squeezed it hard. She jolted at the pain, but the sensations he built in her had her dizzy.

The images of the man and woman writhing in sex filled her mind as Manix's voice filled her head. "The princess tried to escape, but the unicorn's grip was firm. Lightning struck a nearby tree. In the flash, the unicorn became a man, a warlock gripping his princess."

The lights flashed, and the actor, who was the unicorn, appeared as a caped warlock who held the woman naked before him. As the haunting and melodic music built, they danced together. The tune echoed in Evie's mind as the actors danced like they made love.

Manix gripped her head and turned it till he kissed her full on the mouth. The music, his hands, his mouth, it all consumed her. His tongue demanded her reaction, and she was only able to respond. The sensations flowed over her body in waves, building to a crescendo.

Manix's hand shifted and clamped over her sex, making lightning bolts burst within her. He held her before him as he whispered, "Evie, open yer eyes. Watch, my dear." Evie could only comply.

The warlock lifted the woman and laid her on the ground as Manix's voice came to her. "He captured her, taking her heart. Keeping it locked away, so her love was only his, forever."

The man came over to the woman, and the couple undulated on the floor as lights flashed around them.

Manix lifted Evie into his arms and carried her out the back door.

Chapter 6

With Evie in a sensual daze, Manix carried her down a hall and shouldered his way into a room.

He stood a moment, and her eyes adjusted to the light. Candles lit the room. Hundreds of them filled the dresser on the bedside table, all flickering in the night. Against the wall, a nineteenth-century canopied bed draped in black silk glittered in the candlelight. Manix's heady musk scent filled the room, making her dizzy. He strode to the bed and laid her on it, his body soon following as he covered her, kissing her thoroughly.

Manix caressed her cheek as he kissed her hard. His body came flush, and his arousal rubbed full against her sex. He sat back, stripping his jacket and then his shirt, his chest muscles shifting with the movement. When he came back over her, her hands roamed his chest, marveling at its smoothness, the only hair a patch in the middle.

Manix's hand moved to her sides and shifted under her shirt as she rose and allowed him to take it off. She fell back, brushing her hair around her head.

Manix sat back, grinning. "God, ye look like a Fae. Yer hair fanned out, set against yer pale, beautiful skin, a temptress." He trailed his fingers down her chest, stopping at her bra, unlatching the front hook, and pulling it away as she shifted.

He cupped both breasts as he whispered, "A Siren,

like in the mythology, lures in her man. Her main goal is to provide whatever his heart's desire is." His hands trailed over her hip, grabbed her underwear, and stripped them from her body.

She moved her hands, covering her chest, and Manix grabbed the wrists, gripping her hard. "Never cover yerself from me, Evie. Ever."

Manix covered her, rubbing his chest against hers. "By the gods, Evie, ye tease me."

He kissed her as his hands unbuttoned his jeans. He took them off without taking his lips off hers. His shaft rubbed against her leg as he pushed over her, bringing them together. Heat infused her as his tongue danced with hers. His hand nudged between them, rubbing her sex; wet warmth spread as her heart beat a quick rhythm. He brushed her, and waves of delight flowed over her fast, too fast. Her heart sped up as he rose above her.

Her mind screamed. *Too fast, too fast!*

She pushed against him, backing away against the headboard, as tears filled her eyes.

He crawled, following her. "Evie, ye are mine." He edged over her and gripped her face in his hand.

Her mind was all a jumble, but the only certainty she knew was the word. "No!"

Manix spoke through clenched teeth. "No one denies me."

A tear trailed down her cheek and then fell on his hand. "I'm not denying ye. Manix, maybe for ye, this is fine. But for me, it's all too much, too fast."

Manix stared at his hand, where the tear hit. His breath came in huge gulps.

He tilted his head, and his breathing came easier.

His grip eased. "Evie, the gods are right. I can only take ye as fate sees fit."

He gathered her in his arms, and they lay there naked.

He uttered as he kissed her head, "Ye may take time, Evie. But know this: I will always hold yer heart as mine."

She turned into his arms, his firm embrace bringing her comfort.

Manix's hand shifted under her chin until her eyes met his. "This is yer first time?" He breathed. "I thought…" then shook his head.

Evie blushed at the memory. "Well, I almost, once."

She shook her head as Manix shifted till their faces met. "I will teach ye what pleasure is. Come, my princess, and let yer king show ye."

Manix's lips brushed hers softly. His fingers trailed her breasts, circling, tickling them a little. She sucked in a breath, and his hand gripped her breast as his kisses took her to new heights. His thumb flicked her nipple, and the pain came with a heated sensation. His mouth went to it, and he suckled, bringing the pain back as his other hand gripped the other breast hard.

Evie arched into his assault on her senses. His lips first on one breast, then the other. He came back to her lips as his hand took hers and brought it to his shaft, showing her how to grip him. He guided her hand, pumping him as he kissed her hard. When he relocated his hand to her juncture, she kept the rhythm on him. He groaned as he slid his fingers over her bud, spreading her juices. She bucked as tingles spread through her.

Manix's voice came to her. "That's it, sweet princess, bring me to ecstasy." His hand moved away, gripping hers as he guided her, pumping harder as he panted. She lay there, the sensual sensations faded, but his hand held hers, moving over him. He froze and groaned as wetness covered their hands where they gripped him. Manix huffed once, then again.

After wiping his hands, he took her in his arms. "That, my queen, is passion."

Evie lay in his arms, not sure what to think. She'd felt a little passion. But what they did left her wanting, craving something she couldn't reach. She sighed and curled into his embrace.

****

A jostling woke Evie. Manix stood over her, fully dressed, holding a cloak over his arm, the other stretched out to her. "Come, my queen, I'll take ye home."

She sat up fully clothed. How had Manix done that without waking her? She must be exhausted.

When she stood, he wrapped her in a deep black cloak. "A gift for my queen." He kissed her cheek as warmth surrounded her.

Manix turned them to the door, walking through it.

He took her past the stage with another play on. It was a comedy as the actors yelled and the crowd laughed. Soon, the gathering faded away, and the quiet of Edinburgh at night enveloped them. She seemed hazy as they walked in the cold night air, but she felt warm tucked in Manix's cloak.

At the door to her flat, he brushed a kiss on her head and opened the door for her.

She went inside but paused in the doorway.

"Manix, I never found out. How did yer story end?"

Manix had started to walk away but turned at her question, his eyes leveling with hers. "The princess gave her soul to the devil to become a swan and fly away, escaping her capture. But her heart the warlock kept for him alone. She might be free, but never be able to love again."

A shiver passed over Evie. She stood momentarily and pondered his unicorn tale's sad, tragic ending. She lifted her head to ask him about it, but he was already gone.

****

Manix stood in the shadows as Evie stayed on her doorstep. Had she realized what she'd done? Her tear fell on his bare skin, a mating ritual step. He breathed deeply, and the one inside growled in approval.

The ritual steps ran through his mind again. He'd scented her during their dinner—intimacy another step. He'd come close this night, but her fright and inexperience kept him from possessing her.

At first, her mishap angered him. When the reality of her memory flashed, it all became clear. She was a virgin, pure and unspoiled just for him.

She'd yet to declare her love, and he waited. Yet another step. She must be the first to do so. He needed to heal her only once. After she saw him in his true form, all the steps would be complete, and Evie would bind herself to him for all eternity as his soul mate. The gods spoke in his favor. Evie would be his regardless of her stupid Fae boy.

Chapter 7

As she snuggled into the cloak, Evie shuffled into the kitchen, intent on some warm coffee. A shiver racked her body. She needed to get warm.

Ewan followed her. "Sis, ye ill? All wrapped up. It's summer, hot outside."

Kat sat at the bar facing her. "Evie, is that sweat on yer brow?"

Evie wiped her forehead, and sure enough, perspiration covered her hand. She shrugged and poured water into the kettle, then plugged it in.

Kat eyed her up and down. "New cloak? It's nice."

Doug lay on the couch, flipping a gold coin.

Evie gathered cups, four in all. As was their morning ritual, Ewan grabbed the coffee press, coffee, and tea bags, helping her.

When he set them down, he turned to her. "Why don't ye just take off the cloak, Evie?"

She grabbed the edges as the thought of removing it chilled her more. "No! I must wear it."

Ewan reached for the cloak. "Come, sis, ye drip with sweat, and yer face is red."

When Ewan's hand touched the fabric, sparks flew.

He jumped back, holding his hand. "Damn cloak shocked me!"

Kat sat stunned. "Were those flashes?"

Doug flipped the coin and caught it. "Must be

static electricity."

Ewan rubbed his hand. "Not this. No, this is something else."

Evie focused on the kettle, hoping it'd heat faster.

Her brother interrupted her thoughts. "The cloak, Evie, take it off."

She shrugged. "Not now."

Evie sensed Ewan gather energy. Would he pull a spell or cast something onto her? His power built as he grabbed her cloak and pulled it back hard. She tried gripping it, and with a shock of energy, the fabric came away from her body. The force of it flung Ewan on his rear end.

Evie shook herself as Kat glanced between the two. "Was that energy between ye both? Cool!"

Ewan stood holding the cloak. "Not cool, Kat." He shook out the garment as the chill faded from Evie's body. The kettle whistled, and she focused on pouring hot water into the coffee press and cups.

Ewan rifled through the coat. "The cloak, Evie. Where did it come from?" His hand came free from the first pocket, holding two lanyards with the all-access passes to an arts festival she'd wanted to attend. Where had those come from?

Kat jumped from her stool. "Damn, passes to The Hidden Door Project!" Her eyes met Evie's. "A surprise? Ye will take me?"

Evie, feeling much better, smiled. "Aye, Kat. Surprise!" Well, that covered her confusion soundly and kept her promise to Kat to take her out.

With a yelp, Kat took off for her bedroom.

Evie set Ewan's cup on the bar, picked up hers and Doug's, and strode to the couch, handing Doug his.

Maybe if she avoided her brother, he'd not notice her uncertainty.

Doug sat up, taking the cup. "Thanks, Evie."

After checking the other pocket, Ewan's hand came out empty.

His mind speak came to her as she sat beside Doug sipping her coffee. *~The cloak, Evie. Where did ye get it? ~*

Evie ignored him, not wanting to answer. Her desire to anger him rose inside her like nothing she'd experienced.

He strode to her and held it before her, *~Who gave ye the cloak?~*

Emotions washed over her as a different voice spoke in her mind, *~It isn't his, it's mine. Mine to have and keep near my heart. Mine. Take it.~*

Evie reached to grab the garment.

Ewan pulled back, holding it away from her. Desperate to get her coat back, Evie flung her cup aside and tackled Ewan, who sidestepped her as she threw herself on the floor.

Doug chuckled. "She wants her coat, Ewan."

Evie stood, grabbing it again. Ewan shied away, and with a flick of his wrist, the coat burst into flames. In a blink, Ewan stood there, his hand empty.

His voice came firm, magic enhancing his demand. *~The cloak had a spell, a Fae spell. Who gave it to ye?~*

She stood blinking at him as tears gathered. She didn't know, honestly couldn't remember.

Strong arms embraced her as her brother's voice whispered in her ear, "Whatever it is, Evie, we'll fight it together." He held her a moment, and she hiccupped a sigh.

His command came softly, enhanced with power to obey, "Who?"

She shoved back and opened her mouth. Nothing came out. She tried again, and nothing.

Ewan's voice echoed in her head, ~*Ye can't say it, can ye? Damn, that's a powerful spell.*~

His eyes met hers. "Ye can't see yer Fae boy anymore, Evie. The fable, it's ye!"

Doug flipped his coin, and Evie caught it, "Me? Ha! What about ye?" She glanced at the coin, quickly recognizing the symbol stamped into the gold—"E" and "I" inside a heart with a "C" over and a four on top of a heart.

She held it out before him. "East India Trading Company. The date is even stamped on the bottom. Seventeen hundred eighty-seven."

As Ewan tried to grab it, she held the coin close to her body. "Tell me, brother, do ye go around telling everyone ye are a sparrow from yer pirate history books ye read over and over?" She held the coin out, shoving it in his face. "The fable is ye; the *bird* is ye!"

Doug stood and grabbed the coin. "That captain's name would be stupid. No one knew of Captain John Ward nicknamed 'sparrow.' " He rubbed the currency. "Ewan must be someone historically notable and well feared for all time. He grows a beard, long and black, calling himself…"

Ewan cut Doug off. "It's not me we have to worry about. It's Evie."

Evie didn't want to admit anything, especially to Ewan.

Ewan grabbed her arm as she moved past them

both, whispering only to her, "Evie, I only worry for ye."

Evie pulled her arm away and sniffed. "Ye smell like dead fish."

Ewan smirked and sniffed. "And God, Evie, bathe. Ye smell." The familiar game was a welcome break in the tension between them. As children, they'd played outside till they both stank and then had to take turns in the bath. The teasing was part of the game of "who smelt the worst."

As Ewan turned, Evie grabbed his hand. "Thank ye, brother, but I can handle it."

****

Showered with a new set of clothes, robbed from Kat's closet, Evie and Kat both strode into the crowd at The Hidden Door Project. Being a Saturday, people packed the place. Tents with different acts crowded the street as they neared the main building. Kat stopped at each one, marveling at every show—first, the jugglers, the same street performers Evie recognized from yesterday. Wait, a memory clicked into her mind. Yesterday, when she came here with Manix.

The next tent had singers but no instruments. Yesterday, they had instruments as well. The next tent Kat dragged her to had a lone actor, who was soon joined by another who winked at the crowd as he announced they had performed an original script.

Evie only half paid attention, her eyes constantly cast about, looking for Manix. If he had brought her here last night, he certainly would have been here today.

Kat nudged her. "Ale and food?" Evie nodded as her gaze roamed the crowd.

Another memory slid into her mind. Carl and Ria walking with them. Carl bragged about Manix being the large donor that kept the event going. Certainly, someone of Manix's distinction would be here on the festival's busiest day.

She bumped into another person and turned to find Carl and Ria before her.

She grinned. "Hey, guys, have ye seen Manix?"

Carl barked a laugh. "Goth girl spoke to us."

Ria gaped at her outfit. "Not goth girl anymore. She's wearing *pastels*!"

Evie eyed her outfit, light pink jeans with a pale blue baggy tee shirt. Kat had said it offset her lighter hair beautifully, yet she still wore her black combat boots.

Evie dismissed the insult, interested in finding Manix. "Have either of ye seen Manix?"

Carl brushed past her. "Why would we see him?"

Ria followed and turned, whispering as she passed, "Manix is out of yer league. Go back to yer ghosts."

Well, that was strange. Yesterday they'd been so nice. Evie stared as the crowd swallowed them. A chill spread down her back. Was yesterday only a dream? What about Manix?

A hand on her shoulder startled her, and she turned to face Kat, who handed her an ale, "Ale?"

Kat juggled items in her hands, then handed Evie meat on a stick. Kat bit into hers, the juices running down her chin.

Kat slurped her drink and beamed. "Fun, isn't it?"

Evie drank ale from her cup and bit into her meat as she stared at the main building for the event. Something teased her memory: the building, a bedroom.

Kat finished off hers and eyed Evie, who handed her meat to Kat and kept her drink, gulping the rest.

Determined to find Manix or proof he'd been there at all, Evie strode toward the main building as Kat called after her, "Wait up, Evie."

Kat wiped her hands with a napkin and tossed it in a nearby bin as Evie marched to the large building. She elbowed through the front doors and allowed her eyes to adjust. The temporary stage was the same as before. Stagehands moved sets about as people shifted, some entering and some leaving. Evie pushed her way to the backstage area.

A large man in all black stopped her. "Only event organizer passes beyond this point, miss." Evie rolled her eyes and held her badge out for him as Kat caught up, holding her badge for the man. He nodded as he waved them in.

Backstage, they'd been backstage watching a play, his play. He'd carried her through a door into a hall and bedroom.

Evie progressed quickly through the backstage area to the door in the far back. She pushed on it, and it wouldn't budge. She glanced about, checking for another entry. This was the only one in the area.

Last night, Manix took her through this door. She was sure of it. She pushed again, and Kat slammed her body against it, the door giving way with a squeak.

They fell through, but Kat caught Evie, stopping her fall. Evie shook herself and strode down the hall, the third door her focus.

Kat called after her, "Evie..." Evie blocked her out. She had to know, had to see. Was it all a dream?

Couldn't be. She had the lanyards. Her body spoke of sexual awakening. She pushed on the door, which opened, making a dust cloud. Sunlight shone through the windows, the only light in the room. A teacher's desk sat far to her right, a chalkboard behind it. A layer of dust spoke of the timelessness of space, the fact it sat untouched for years.

As she stepped into the room, dust particles captured the light and danced around her as she turned a full circle. Students' desks sat askew, some on their sides but not in a line like a classroom. It wasn't possible, but here the room sat, nothing like it had the night before.

Someone brushed her arm as Kat's voice came to her. "Evie, come on, let's go."

Evie jerked her arm away and strode to the teacher's desk. "It was here. A nineteenth-century bed with full drapes in black satin, candles, and musk scent." She shoved past the students' desks and stood in the middle of the room, waving her hands as she spoke. "He was here. We were here. It was a bedroom, sexy and alluring. A temptress, he called me."

Evie turned and faced her longtime friend with tears in her eyes. "I didn't dream it. I was here."

Kat came to her and took her hand, patting it. "I'm sure, Evie. But for now, can we go?" Kat pulled them to the exit, and Evie let her take the lead, unsure what to think.

Kat's voice came to her softly, "Come, Evie, let's go home."

At the door, Evie looked at the dusty schoolroom. "I'm going to find out what Manix is up to. He has some things to answer for."

****

That night, Evie fell into a fitful sleep where images of demons plagued her dreams. Monsters wrapped in black cloaks chased her through the old schoolhouse as dust made her cough. Every turn she took, another black mass rose before her. Evie woke restless and tired. Even in her dreams, her doubts manifested in her mind.

Evie rose and dressed in all-black, hoping to find solace in her clothing, not Kat's. The rest of the flat slept, and she liked being alone. Wanting to get out, she grabbed both gems from her dresser, the Iona stone Manix gave her in one pocket and the teardrop gemstone Aodhán made from her tear in another.

Running through the flat, she burst from the door to the outside, taking in large gulps of fresh air that woke her senses and refreshed her.

Today was her day off, but she made her way to the Grass Market anyway.

Her ghost friends warmly greeted her along the way. Nal called out at the toll booth, and she waved. Maureen at the bakery now dress shop offered her a pastry, but she didn't have the desire to play along today.

She passed Maggie's bar and progressed farther into the Friar's Kirkyard, hoping to find Manix. She wandered the rows and rows of graves, passing one then another of the wizard school tours. None were Manix. She thought about asking, but remembered Manix said he worked alone, not for any tour company.

She settled beside a grave in the middle of the cemetery, finding peace and quiet. Even though many ghosts floated about, none seemed to notice her.

Evie curled her legs in, wrapping her arms around her knees. Why had Brigid gifted her with Fae powers to begin with?

As a youth, she'd asked many times, and Brigid's reply was always the same, "Ye were gifted already. I only enhance what is there. Ye are needed for something far bigger than ye know."

What was she needed for? The Stone of Hope she and Ewan found in a statue in Egypt of the thirties? That wasn't something "Far bigger than ye know."

Doubts flashed through her mind. Was she good enough for whatever task Brigid seemed to have in mind? Was she good enough for anything?

Her stones warmed, and she placed her hands in her pockets, holding each one as she rested her head on her knees.

Her mind turned to Aodhán, her Fae boy, now a man. The teardrop stone sat in her hand, a reminder of his care. He'd not come to her for two nights in a row. He said to look for him in her dreams. But lately, evil plagued and chased her.

Manix. What of him? The festival and the bedroom, was it all a dream? A figment of her imagination? And the cloak Ewan claimed held a Fae spell. How had she gotten it? Evie huffed hard. What was wrong with her?

Brown sandals and a rough brown robe came into her vision. When she looked up, a friar's ghost floated before her.

He grinned as he asked, "May I join ye?" He waved to the space beside her on the gravestone.

She nodded, dropping her feet and allowing them to rest on the ground.

The clergyman sat there a moment as the silence stretched between them. Evie relaxed into solitude, her mind clearing a bit. The ghost sat, not saying anything else, but his presence soothed her, and calm washed over her.

Things in her mind sorted out and became clearer. Aodhán was good and cared for her. Manix, well, he had some explaining to do when she found him. Maybe he was a ghost and vanished for good? She laughed at that one. Manix was no ghost.

The Fae fable, Stone of Doubt, ran through her mind—the riddle of a swan captured to thwart true loves from coming together. It couldn't be her. She'd not found her true love, not yet.

She turned to the ghost. "Was there something ye needed?"

He smiled as he glanced at her. "No, my dear. It wasn't me who needed something, but ye."

Evie sat back. "Me?"

The friar patted her hand, the actual touch of the ghost soothing her. "Aye, and I think ye found it, Evie."

Evie glanced down as his voice took on an ethereal tone. "Remember, Evie, there is a sacredness in tears. They are not the mark of weakness but of power. The power of tears shall quell any person, my girl. The people around ye love and care for ye. Look to them for assurance."

The quote from the Fae fable, the Stone of Doubt—he'd spoken it.

Her head shot up, and the friar was gone. Glancing around the yard, she noted all the ghosts had left. Dusk settled on the hill. She'd been here longer than she thought. But the friar's comfort and statement brought her hope. Hope. She just needed hope.

Chapter 8

That night, sleep came easily for Evie. She'd come home from the kirkyard with a clearer mind and heart. Alone in the flat, a simple dinner of warm stew set the perfect mood for a good night's rest.

Her head hit the pillow, and soon, restful bliss wrapped her mind in a soft cushion.

Soon, her dream world opened, and she stood in the throne room in the Fae realm, Aodhán's home, Broemere Castle, dressed in her Fae gown.

When she thought of him, warm arms embraced her from behind as Aodhán's breath tickled her ear. "Mmm, gardenias, yer own sweet scent. I missed ye, Evie."

She wrapped her arms around his and leaned back into his embrace. "I missed ye as well."

He turned her in his arms. "Ye did? Why didn't ye call?"

His hand brushed her hair from her face. "I tried to come to ye. But the way. Something blocked me."

Evie shivered as a chill crawled up her spine. Images from her previous dreams flashed in her mind. The monsters wrapped in black cloaks chased her through the old schoolhouse as dust made her cough. Every turn she took, another black mass rose before her.

She shook them off, casting them from her mind as

she focused on the man before her, Aodhán.

His smile grew. "Come, I'll show ye the kingdoms today. Then we'll stop at our special spot."

He took her hand and headed for the balcony overlooking the ocean's cliff. At the edge, he started to step off.

Evie grabbed his hand with both hers tugging back.

Aodhán turned as he chuckled. "Sorry, Evie, I forget myself." He came to her with her hands before him, kissing them. Sensations floated through her body. He bent and kissed her lips as her world tilted a little—kind of like when she traveled through a portal.

When Aodhán lifted his head, he stepped back, holding her hand. When Evie's eyes left him, her focus went down, and they floated over the ocean. She yelped and grabbed his hand with both of hers. They flew!

Aodhán took her into his embrace and held her to his side. "Not to worry, Evie. I make us float. Flying is the easiest way to travel the kingdoms of my world quickly." Her eyes traveled his form, and from his back, butterfly-shaped wings fluttered fast. Their luminescent glow glinted in a wave of movement.

Aodhán turned them to the right, and they flew fast over the ocean toward another large cloud. Another castle floated in the distance. The same blue-green dragon she'd seen before flew above it. This castle was pink and smaller than Broemere Castle.

Aodhán tilted his head. "Morrigan's home."

He turned them back, and they flew past Broemere Castle, its blue crystal winking in the sun.

They slowed near another cluster of clouds, and Evie made out golden gates like an entrance. A man and woman moved to go through the gates. Her eyes must be playing tricks on her. Before her stood Colin, her da, but in historical clothing, looking exactly like the portrait that hung in Dunstaffnage Castle.

She called out, "Da! Da, I'm here!"

The man turned, and his expression registered confusion. The woman with him held his arm like a couple, but she wasn't her ma. This woman had darker hair and was a little taller.

Evie turned, trying to fly toward the gates and her da.

Aodhán pulled on her hand, moving them away from the kingdom. "Evie, that kingdom is forbidden to ye."

Aodhán's pull felt like he dragged her away. Her desire to go to her da was so strong.

She pulled again. "No, Aodhán, he's my da."

Aodhán took her chin and kissed her. His command that she focus on him came strongly to her. "He isn't yer da, Evie."

Her world tilted again as if they proceeded through a portal. They floated, landing on the cliff edge they'd been on the last time she was in this realm. Her view was of the lake with a waterfall. The sky had changed to dusk, and the lake before them glittered in the golden rays. The sky shifted, and warm sunlight faded into night as the moon rose above them.

Aodhán took her into his arms. "This, Evie, is the Moon Garden. A sacred place in the Fae realm."

Evie glanced at him. "We've been here before."

A smile grew on his face. "Aye, we have. This time, though, we have more time."

Aodhán raised his hand, Evie's eyes following. He twirled his fingers over their heads, and their clothing disappeared.

Evie shivered, and Aodhán took her closer into his arms, his warmth spreading.

Evie's mind recalled the vision the last time they were there, and Aodhán's grin widened as his naked body brushed against hers.

Evie giggled. "Ye didn't rip yer shirt off this time."

Aodhán covered her with his body. "Clothing fading from view was yer request?"

Evie laughed. "Aye, that it was."

Aodhán bent, laving her nipple as his hand cupped her breast. Evie threw her head back, sighing into the sky.

As he growled, he shifted, picked her up, and lay on the cliff's ledge. Her back rested on a pillow of soft leaves and moss, just as she had before.

He covered her, sliding their bodies together. The velvety feel of his warm skin against her sent sparks through her body. She clamped her legs as warmth settled there. Aodhán kissed her madly, their tongues swirling in a dizzying dance.

Aodhán shifted her leg to the side, and he rubbed against her, his rod rubbing against her, spreading warmth. He cupped her breast and suckled the nipple, sending jolts of awareness through her. He rocked and slid against her as he returned to kissing her. She rocked with him, craving his touch, his heat. He shifted her other leg till he settled over her. His kisses became maddening as he reached between them and flicked his finger over her nub. Evie cried out as shockwaves rocked her body.

Aodhán breathed into his kiss. "Did ye like that?"

Breathless, Evie could only manage a sigh as her

response.

Aodhán's hand moved again, covering her, and his finger slid in. The thrusts of his tongue match the thrusts of his finger. Something rose inside her, an energy she'd not felt before.

Her breaths panted as Aodhán rose above her. "Evie, I must have ye!"

His hand shifted between them, and he pressed against her. She knew not what she craved.

She only wanted him. "Aodhán, please," was all she could say.

He slid into her in one long sigh. Her body stretched, then a pinch, and Aodhán kissed her hard, "Evie, I love ye."

He stayed seated a moment, keeping his body joined with hers. He kissed her again, slowly, as his body rocked against hers.

Warmth spread over her, and that energy built again. Evie returned his kisses with vigor as that craving took over her body again.

Aodhán shifted and pushed harder within her. Heat consumed her body and filled her with each thrust. Tingling started where they joined as Aodhán pushed faster, harder. That energy spread over her. The heat, the friction, and the things he did to her consumed her.

A force built inside her as Aodhán continued to press into her. Again and again, as the energy grew till it filled her body, her mind, unable to bear it anymore, something burst within her, forcing her to cry out. Stars exploded behind her eyelids as Aodhán kissed her. His body continued its onslaught to her senses. Thrust after thrust, he carried her over the boundary of existence into a world that was only theirs. He froze over her, arched, and screamed her name to the heavens. Wetness flooded her, and fulfillment overcame her.

Panting, Aodhán withdrew from her and took her in his arms. They both lay trying to catch their breaths as sweat glistened on their bodies.

Aodhán gathered her in his arms as they lay naked under the moonlight. "Evie, do ye know how I feel about ye?"

She stirred, not wanting to move but curious at his inquiry. "Mm, like I do about ye? Love?"

He turned his head till their gazes met, his fingers touching her chin, "Evie, things are different in the Fae realm. Ye must understand that before I proceed."

Evie nodded, her focus clear on him now. He had something important to discuss. She took a deep breath, trying to loosen the butterflies fluttering in her chest.

Aodhán kissed her lips. "I sense yer unease. Please, Evie, be calm. What I plan is something I think ye will like, take great joy in." Now, he had her attention. Those flutters turned to total mush.

Aodhán kissed her lightly as his breath brushed her lips when he spoke, "Evie, I have a surprise for ye."

Her heart soared, and she kissed him. "Surprise? Can I have it now?"

He chuckled and set her back, his eyes intent on hers. "Not now. Tomorrow night."

Evie's eyes traveled over his face; his hair, and returned to his bright blue eyes, "Why wait?"

He kissed her neck and sighed. "I need time to prepare. The day after tomorrow, meet me here."

Evie rested her head on his shoulder and held on to her Fae lover, Aodhán. His heart beat steadily against her ear, his warmth enveloped her, and sleep soon found her.

****

Aodhán returned to his bedroom after leaving Evie in the human realm, tucked into her bed, clothed in her Fae gown. He paced as excitement filled him.

Aodhán went to his chest and pulled out a silver jeweled necklace. The pendant glittered in the sunlight and held the sign of eternity on top of ivy leaves. Over that sat a five-pointed star made of clear Fae crystal, the most powerful. His immortality. The only item he could give to anyone to form a bond lasting for eternity.

His mother flashed into the room. "Ye didn't. Ye couldn't have. Aodhán, what is wrong with ye? There's a law against a human and Fae coming together."

He ignored his mother and strode to the window overlooking the ocean.

Sensing her frustration, he barked at her, unable to hold back, "The Fae law applies to humans without Fae powers. Evie is different. Ye know this. Part Fae herself, born from a line of seers that lay hidden for generations." He huffed, "Mother, ye only mentioned the law to rile me."

Bridgid came beside him. "Okay, she's part Fae but doesn't know it. But what of the prophecy? The realm, yer future kingdom?"

He turned to his mother. "My whole existence has been about this kingdom, this realm, its people. I have served for a long time, ye have served for a long time, my grandparents have served even longer."

He yelled the last, "The fight for this realm took my father! This I do for me! She's my fated love, my soul mate!"

He sensed his mother wanted to yell back but held

it in.

She wrapped her arms around him. "Ye learned too much from the humans. They've shown ye a way to have yer love and still, in the long haul, keep yer commitments to the Fae."

His ma patted his cheek. "Giving yer immortality to her, making ye mortal. The way to a life with yer love." She held him at arm's length. "Ye found a way around it, like Laird Colin MacDougall."

She shook her head. "Aodhán, I hope ye know what ye do. Ye put yerself at such a risk. Mortal means ye could die easier."

He stepped from his ma's arms. "To be without Evie. To live and watch her grow old, then die without sharing her lifespan with her. That's a hell I do not wish for."

Wiping a tear from her face she smiled. "I am happy for ye, scared, but happy."

Chapter 9

Evie dragged herself into the flat, tossed her bag on the floor, and fell on the couch. She was finally lying down, with her feet up in relief. The lunch shift during tourist peak season was hell, and weekends were even more challenging.

Kat burst into the common room. "I've waited for you the whole day! A package came for you." She set the large black box on the coffee table as Evie opened one eye. A gift for her?

Kat handed her a piece of paper. When she took it, the heavy vellum caught her attention. She flipped it over, and a wax seal held it shut. Her finger ran over the blood-red seal, a dragon in full flight.

Curiosity peeked, she sat up and broke the seal. Heavy musk wafted from the paper as she opened the letter. In a curvy script, the note read:

My princess,

Join me this weekend for events and a costume ball celebrating the success of yet another victorious year for The Hidden Door Project. Dress for travel, bring the costume, and pack an overnight bag. Essentials only. I have many surprises for you. Your escort arrives at three pm. Don't be late.

I look forward to welcoming you to my ancestral castle.

Manix

Evie ran her fingers over the raised ink blotted here and there, looking like one of her ma's historical scrolls.

Kat leaned over her shoulder. "Damn, Evie. It's only Wednesday. He's invited ye for a weekender with a costume ball in a castle." She nudged her. "Open the box. Let's see the costume!"

Evie set the note aside as she shifted on the couch and pulled the large black ribbon tied around a box large enough to hold two costumes. When she lifted the lid, the scent of patchouli rose from the black tissue inside. When Evie opened the folded tissue, black feathers sat underneath. At first glance, she thought it might be a mask, but when she picked it up, she held a boned bodice. When she stood, the garment came fully from the box, revealing a dress of black feathers. Underneath sat a set of black wings. She set aside the gown and picked up the extensions. Beneath those were high heels decorated with feathers, so the sides matched the wings.

Kat's whistle filled the room. "Fancy that, a black swan!" Her eyes met Evie's. "Wow, he called you a princess."

Evie set the wings aside. "I don't know, Kat. What if I don't want to see Manix anymore?"

Kat picked up the dress, twirling as she held it before her. "So, go to the ball, eat, drink, and be merry. Then tell him you only want to be friends."

Kat stopped eyeing the note. "Did he say where his ancestral castle was? It mentions travel and an overnight bag."

Evie picked up the letter as the heavy musk came to her, making her dizzy. "No, but I guess it doesn't matter." She set the note aside. "I can always call a car share if I want to leave."

Kat set the dress down and picked up the note. "Three; it's already two. In an hour, Evie, your escort arrives! Ye must get ready!"

****

An hour later, the bell rang, and an excited Kat answered. Two men in black suits stood in the doorway. Beyond them, a limousine sat in the street. Evie stood in her bedroom doorway, apprehension rising.

She glanced at Aodhán's teardrop gem on the desk next to Manix's Iona stone. She gathered energy and called both stones to her. Aodhán's flew to her, but Manix's didn't budge. She pocketed Aodhán's and gathered more energy, forcing Manix's stone to her. It nearly flew past her, but she caught it, pocketed it, and strode forward with her small bag. Kat grabbed the black box from the coffee table and handed it to one man. The other took her bag, freeing her hands.

He handed her bag to the first man and held out his hand. "This way, Ms. MacDougall. Laird Skene doesn't like anyone to be late." His thick brogue sounded like someone from deeper in the highlands. Evie took his hand and followed him to the limo.

When she glanced back at Kat, she stood in the doorway with her hand to her ear like a phone mouthing, "Call me!"

The Scot opened the back door and waved Evie into the back seat. She slid in, feeling out of place in her ripped jeans, baggy tee, and combat boots. Manix had said to dress for travel. Would they drive her the whole way in the limo? She hoped not.

Before the escort closed the door, he pointed to the assortment of items in the car, "There's champagne chilled, cheese and crackers, and the telly's connected to a satellite, but we won't be in the car long."

Evie glanced up. "We won't? Where are we going?"

The man smiled. "Ye'll see soon. Welcome, Ms. MacDougall." He closed the door. The sound of both men getting into the car with slammed doors were the only sounds she heard. The engine revved and soon sped off to God knows where.

****

The limo ride wasn't long. Upon exiting the limo, Evie found herself outside of Edinburgh on a private airstrip before a small jet, complete with a red carpet leading to the stairs. Manix could afford all this? His ancestral castle needed a plane ride to get to?

During the car ride, she named the two men, Hamish and Connor, after the wharf lads who did odd jobs around Dunstaffnage Castle over the years.

The first, the one she named Hamish, held his hand out to her and led her to the plane. "Where do we go?"

He patted her hand. "To Laird Skene's castle in Ireland."

She climbed the stairs and glanced over her shoulder.

The second, the one she called Connor, followed her with her bag and the black box. "It's a three-hour flight to Donegal Airport. There's a place inside to rest if ye want."

The plane itself had two seats behind the cockpit, and beyond, a pulled-back curtain revealed a bed that called to Evie.

Connor shifted past her, placing her bag and the box beside the bed. "Rest, if ye like." The cabin smelled of the same heady musk Manix's note had, and weariness overcame Evie. She nearly stumbled onto the bed.

Someone covered her with a blanket, and Connor's voice was the last she heard. "Laird Skene will be happy. His queen is on her way."

****

A little over four hours later, a rested Evie emerged from the limo and stood before a large sand-colored stone castle. A picture of a French chateau from her ma's history books flashed in her mind. The escort she named Connor nodded her forward as he carried her bag and box behind her.

As she approached the large double wooden doors, they swung open, and Manix stood inside the entry. The wind blew in as she entered, ruffling his loose hair. He stood still in his black suit, waiting till she came to him. A servant stood beside him with a tray. Her eyes followed Connor as he passed her items to another servant and turned to leave. The castle doors closed behind him, the thump echoing throughout the hall.

Her gaze returned to Manix, who beamed. "Evie. Welcome to my home." He waved to the tray. "Please accept my hospitality and partake in a ceremonial tradition. Eat bread and drink wine from my home."

Evie nodded, recognizing the tradition her ma had commented on from history. The old tradition seemed something Manix was fond of. She pulled a piece of bread, ate it, and washed it down with red wine, heady and rich. Another maid appeared with a bowl and towel.

Evie blinked as Manix spoke, "To wash yer hands with. It's part of the ritual."

She dipped her hands and dried them.

When she finished, he stepped forward and took her hands in his. "I am happy ye are here, in my ancestral home." He kissed the back, never taking his eyes off hers. "Please freshen up in yer room. Dinner is at seven-thirty." He released her, and the maid who'd held a tray stood before her empty-handed. She led her away, and they entered a grand room like the Great Room at her home, Dunstaffnage Castle.

As she climbed the stairs, Manix's eyes followed. "Evie, seven-thirty sharp. Don't be late."

At the top, they turned left, moved down a hall, and to the door on the left.

Upon entering the room, Evie glanced around as a photo from one of her ma's history books flashed in her mind. Her room was a perfect replica of a nineteenth-century woman's boudoir. A king-size bed dominated the room. Its draping canopy made a grand statement. A set of decorative chairs sat before an ornate fireplace, and beyond that, a set of opened double doors led to a balcony where the ocean spread out beyond the manicured lawn.

Another maid came through the door carrying clothes over her arm. "Laird Skene says to dress for dinner and join him in the dining hall."

She set the clothing on the bed and left the room. Well, so much for a warm welcome. Evie fingered the fabric—fine black silk. She lifted the items, and sure enough, it was a black silk dress that fell long. Under were heels. She glanced about and found her bag by the door. She went to pick it up, and beyond that door was a vast bathroom. She flicked on the lights, and a sunken tub sat in the center with a wall-length vanity to her right. She blew a laugh. Kat would die if she were here now. Evie shrugged and figured she'd take Kat's advice—eat, drink, and be merry.

****

Clad in the dress with her hair down in long waves, complete with heels, Evie stared at herself in the mirror. She looked mature, like a woman rather than a college kid. She liked it, a woman.

Her cell phone binged, and she picked it up from the nightstand—a text from Kat.

—*So, where is his castle?* —

Evie went to the balcony, turned, lifted the phone, and took a selfie of the sprawling grounds, including the balcony's stone opening.

She typed, —*Slumming on Tory Island. Flew in a private jet drinking champagne.*—

Evie smirked as she typed more —*I'm to be a princess at the ball in a fancy castle.*— She giggled as she clicked send.

Dots appeared, and the reply came back — *Seriously? Dude, don't lose your shoe!*—

—*I won't!*— Evie clicked send and strode back into the room, noting the time on her cell: seven-fifteen. She needed to go; Manix hated it when anyone was late.

Kat's reply binged. —*Enjoy it before you turn into a pumpkin and tell Manix you only want to be friends.*—

Evie grinned at the reply as she placed the phone on the bedside table. Maybe she should give Manix a chance. All the effort he put in this weekend spoke of something more. Spying his Iona stone, Evie picked it up, flipped the stone, and caught it, placing it in the dress pocket. She'd go with the flow and see where it led. Who knows; maybe she could be a princess at a ball.

Evie made her way down the curving staircase into the vast Great Room. French antique furniture spread throughout the room, and in the grand fireplace, a fire danced. Double doors were open to her left, and light spilled into the room. When she came closer, she noted it was the dining hall. Hall was an understatement. When she entered, the long table took up most of the room, but what drew her farther were the open doors at the far end of the hall. A double set of doors opened to a manicured lawn. Unable to resist, she strode there, and the garden sat on a cliff that overlooked the sea much as her room had.

Evie sighed. The castle was exquisite, a perfect copy of a nineteenth-century French castle. Her ma would love it here.

"I hope ye find it to yer liking, Evie." Manix's breath brushed her ear as his body came flush with her back. She jolted but covered it by brushing her hair away from her face. His arm came around her as she turned to him. He also dressed in all black, with his suit pressed to perfection and his hair loose. Manix looked younger, almost carefree.

Manix beamed as he spoke, "My home is called Tór Mór, meaning Great Tower. Welcome to Tory Island, Ireland."

A servant brought wine glasses in a tray. Manix picked one up, handing it to her; he lifted his. "To a fine weekend."

Evie clinked the glasses and took a sip. Red wine, light and crisp, tickled her tongue. Another set of servants entered carrying silver dome-covered plates.

Manix's hand slid from her waist to her free hand. "Come, dinner is served."

The servants set the plates down and stepped back as Manix led her to the other end of the table, where they'd set two places before the roaring fire. She shivered as she sat, and Manix picked up a plaid from the chair and wrapped it around her shoulders. The plaid was one she'd not seen, a green base with red crossing stripes and a purple stripe every other line.

He bent, kissing her ear. "My colors look good on ye." He sat in the chair beside her, scooting it close as Evie set her wine glass down, noting the bottle sat in a bucket on the table.

She reached for the dome covering to see what was for dinner, and Manix covered her hand with his. "What does my queen want for dinner this evening?" Evie pulled her hand back, but Manix took it in his, holding it as his thumb caressed the back.

Evie shrugged. "Whatever ye have served is fine, Manix."

He smirked. "Humor me, Evie. What would ye like?"

Evie thought it over, and the idea of a lobster tail, scallops, large fat shrimp, and homemade bread next to a melted butter cup made her stomach growl, but she tamped it down with a shrug. "Seafood."

Manix waved, and the servants moved forward in unison and removed the domes. Sure enough, what Evie pictured in her mind sat before her in perfect duplication. On Manix's plate sat a large sirloin bleeding rare with nothing else. He grinned as he waved the servants away.

Evie's gaze flew to Manix. "How did ye?"

He cut into his steak. "A wild guess, Evie." He held the piece up. "Enjoy yer meal, my queen." He shoved the whole bite into his mouth and chewed as he groaned.

Evie cut into her lobster, dipped the morsel into the butter, and placed it in her mouth. The tender shellfish burst in her mouth.

They ate together in silence, each enjoying their meal. Occasionally, she'd stare out the window as the sun set over the cliff, enjoying the view and her delicious meal. The lighter red wine paired well with the seafood. She truly enjoyed herself.

Finished, Manix sat back as he held his wine glass. His servants entered and wordlessly cleared the plates. One filled her wine glass and placed the near-empty bottle in the bucket. Each servant disappeared as quietly as they appeared.

Manix sipped his wine as he stared at her. "Our deep connection with the universe often involves relating ourselves to our shared elements. And of all the entities we share is this planet, its stones. Kings, magicians, shamans, and fortune tellers have used them since the beginning of time." He set his wine glass down and waved his hands together in a circle. When he opened them, he revealed a green square gemstone.

He held it in the firelight as he spoke, "Their energies, magical or psychical, seem to enrapture. How people have used them for rituals—stones capture the imaginations as symbols." His eyes focused on hers as he winked. "As brilliant treasures cloaked in stories and myths."

He tossed the stone in the air, and when he caught it, the stone was blue. "They are merely pieces of this planet. Yet, into them, people have deposited their purest fantasies and metaphors. For this reason alone, stones are magical."

"Take, for example, the diamond." Manix twisted his hand, and a large, round, clear gemstone appeared. Evie marveled at his sleight-of-hand tricks. He seemed to have mastered the art. The large stone was likely glass, but she sat forward, taken in by his act.

He held it out toward her. "The diamond, perhaps the most valuable of stones and certainly the strongest, carrying the most beautiful name. Adamant. The word comes from the Latin meaning 'unbreakable, unconquerable.' "

Manix rolled the jewel on the table. "In the Middle Ages, diamonds were considered the tears of the gods. For this reason, many used them as amulets of good fortune during war." He cupped his hands over the gem and pressed them together hard.

When he opened it, a clear teardrop gem attached to a necklace dropped dangling from his hand. "Beyond being one of the world's most luxurious ornaments, the diamond is still considered an object of multiple symbolism. One that favored mental clarity and spiritual enlightenment."

He folded his hand into his chest, making a fist as he gripped the stone. "Ruby is a stone of love and courage. An aphrodisiac par excellence. The iron and chromium in this valuable stone provide its hypnotizing red color, which happens to be the product of a chemical oxidation process." As he spoke, he brought his fist from his chest, the fingers pumping as if he held a beating heart.

Evie chuckled. "Are ye a geologist now, Manix?"

He grinned. "Maybe. It's no accident that the name of the mineral comes from the Latin word 'simply red.' " He opened his fist, and inside was a red gem shaped like a heart.

"And it's no surprise people used rubies to decorate armor and sheaths of swords. They were sometimes placed in the foundations of buildings to ensure future endurance." He threw the stone to the ground, but before it hit, the stone disappeared. Evie glanced around, wondering how he pulled that one off without the stone hitting the floor or him moving to catch it.

He held his palm out to her, empty. "An Iona stone." Evie's hand went to her pocket where Manix's stone sat. It warmed in her hand.

Manix smiled. "Do ye have the stone I gave ye, Evie?"

As she nodded, she took it out, placing it in his open hand.

He held it up between them. "Iona marble is a serpentine stone from the isle of Iona, possessing pale green patterns of limestone and white or gray marble inclusions." His eyes connected with hers. The stone went out of focus as she stared into his eyes.

"Psychics and spiritual experts say Iona marble's properties give it supernatural powers. Its association with the ruling elements, earth, wind, fire, and water, signify a universal connection." His eyes returned to the stone as did hers, and it returned to focus. "But the magical powers of an Iona stone make it special." He nodded to her hand, and she held it out. Manix placed the stone and closed his hands over hers. The stone warmed as he whispered, "Tell me, Evie, do you know of more Iona stones?"

Evie tried to pull her hand away, and Manix held it firmly. Certainly, he wasn't asking her about the Fae magic stones, which her family kept safe from the evil Fae. Manix couldn't know of those stones. Not many did.

She laughed, making light of a tense moment. "Magic stones, Manix? There're no magic stones." She pulled her hand free, and the stone grew hot. She dropped it on the table. "Likely more of yer magic tricks."

Manix picked up the stone and placed it in her hand again, holding it. "Tricks, maybe, but where's my treat, Evie?" He leaned forward and brushed a kiss on her lips.

He spoke into the kiss, "Ye kept my stone, Evie. Do ye keep my heart?" He deepened the kiss, and his other hand brushed her hair away as he gripped her head. His tongue thrust into her, creating a hypnotic dance with hers. She pulled the stone closer to her as he switched his hands around.

He lifted her and held her in his lap in one quick motion. "Evie, my queen. Be mine. Let's share our hearts."

Sharing her heart. Aodhán flashed in her mind. Her heart belonged to him. She started to slide off Manix's lap. He gripped her, but when she tugged again, he let her go.

Evie held out the stone, offering it to him.

Manix stared at her hand as red flashed over his

face.

His eyes went to hers as a muscle ticked in his cheek. "The stone is yers, my queen. A gift. Keep it."

She turned, moving away, but Manix grabbed her hand. She turned back, facing him.

"Evie, think on it, on us. Ye are my match. I know it."

Evie gripped the stone, turned, and made a hasty retreat from the room—running from herself more than Manix.

****

Manix sat in the dying firelight. He'd tried to show her. Show her his love, their suitability. Her Fae boy blinded her. This weekend would see the end of his grip on her. Manix would ensure she would be his love, princess, and queen. She would bring him all the power. He only had to show her the way.

Chapter 10

Evie woke to satin sheets and the scent of patchouli. She rolled over, reaching for her cell phone on her bedside table, and only encountered more bedding. Evie opened her eyes, and the ornate set of chairs flanked a set of doors that opened to the balcony. It took her a moment to recall where she was, unused to waking in a different place other than her flat or Dunstaffnage Castle, home. Her memory returned— Manix's castle, Tory Island, Ireland.

A maid came through the doors, the same woman from yesterday who carried clothes over her arm, "Laird Skene says to dress and break yer fast with the others in the dining hall."

She set the clothing on the bed and left the room.

Evie called after her, "Ma'am?" The maid's response—Evie's door shutting with a loud click.

Evie hmphed, the same warm welcome as yesterday. She rose and fingered the clothing—fine black silk, like yesterday. She lifted the items, and sure enough, it was a black silk suit with wide-leg pants, a small shirt, and a jacket. Under were heels. Silk and heels again. It must be a favorite of Manix's.

She slid off the bed, moved to pick it up, and turned to the bath. Beyond the door was the vast bathroom she'd used yesterday. She flicked on the lights, and a sunken tub sat in the center with the wall-length vanity. What girl wouldn't love a dip in the tub, primping in the luxurious bath?

****

Dressed in the suit with her hair down in long waves, complete with heels, Evie made her way down the curving staircase into the vast great room. Voices floated to her, and she followed the sound. As the scent of food wafted to her, her stomach growled. She entered the same dining hall as last night, and an extensive food buffet weighed down the long table.

People milled about with drinks and plates. Some were in groups, others as couples, all of varying ages.

Where had all these people come from, and when did they arrive?

The window overlooking the garden and ocean beyond beckoned her. She stirred, moving, and stood in the doorway, taking a deep cleansing breath—then released it.

Manix's voice whispered in her ear, "How was yer rest last night?"

Evie jolted as she turned. "Fine, yers?"

Manix smiled as he took her hand and brought it to his lips, kissing the back. "Lonely. I am happy ye found rest in my home, Evie."

Also dressed in all black, Manix stood still, his suit pressed to perfection and his hair slicked back. Manix seemed years older, but the glint in his eye was the same.

He turned them to the room. "Everyone, may I present Ms. Evie MacDougall, an honored guest this weekend." A murmur of greetings met her as she faced a room of smiling strangers.

Manix led her to the table.

He filled a plate as he spoke, "The ball is this evening, but the guests take their ease today." He handed her a plate. She took it, noting he'd filled it with her favorites—a scone with cream and raspberry preserves. He'd added a rowie, a Scottish breakfast bread Mrs. A made from scratch when Evie was a child. She took a bite of the scone, noting its delicate texture. When she glanced up, Manix held two champagne flutes filled with mimosas. She took the one offered as she swallowed her scone.

Manix clicked them together. "Welcome, I am so happy ye are here, and today has finally arrived." She clinked back, and they both sipped. The tingle of the bubbles made Evie giggle—good food, good drink, and pampered in a castle. Kat was right: enjoy the weekend, then tell him ye only want to be friends.

A man dressed as a servant came to Manix and bent murmuring in his ear.

Manix growled, "He can wait."

The servant shrugged, and Manix turned to Evie, caressing her face. "I have business to attend to. Enjoy yerself today. Relax. The ball starts at six sharp." His hand gripped her chin. "Wear the gown. Evie, don't be late." He kissed her hard and strode from the room.

Evie smirked as Manix strode away. This worked out perfectly—a day without Manix in his billionaire castle. She glanced back out the balcony as a gazebo caught her eye. It sat on the edge of the garden near the cliffside—a perfect place to get away and relax. She walked there, admiring the area as she sipped her drink. She passed other guests, but no one noticed her, and it suited her just fine.

She set her plate and glass on the table at the

pavilion and turned to the castle. The back was stunning. Small half-circle balconies sat at the second and third stories of the home. Each bedroom had its own balcony. The fourth floor had one long balcony, and as her eyes moved up, Manix stood on the top-level staring at her.

She picked up her drink and scone, then lifted her feet to rest on the table. She was not very ladylike, but she wasn't here to be a lady. She was here to relax.

Soon, the idea of doing nothing wore on her. Evie, unused to being idle, stood and paced. She wished she'd brought her book. The latest one she read was about a romance with a vampire. When she turned, the breeze blew off the sea, chilling her. She picked up her plate and glass and turned, coming face to face with two servants, a man and a woman. The woman carried a covered tray, and the man stood with a book and plaid wrap.

The woman set down the dish and took the glass and plate from Evie. "Here, Ms. MacDougall, let me." She set the items down and guided Evie till she sat again. The man wrapped her in the wool wrap and wordlessly set a book before her. The woman placed the covered tray before her and took off the lid. Finger sandwiches and a pot of tea with two cups sat underneath. The maid fixed Evie a cup of tea, light on cream, just as she liked it.

Soon, both servants left her alone without a word. Evie sat back as she picked up the hardcover. When she opened the book, she nearly dropped it. It was the same book Evie had read before, the vampire romance.

When she glanced back at the castle, there were no crowds, and she sat alone on the cliffside. Evie curled up and read her book, content to spend the day alone.

"Teatime. How lovely." Evie started and turned. Manix stood just outside the gazebo.

He waved to the table. "May I?"

Evie sat up and nodded.

Manix stepped up. As he sauntered by her, he brushed his hand along her shoulders.

He sat beside her, smiling. "Will ye make me a cup?"

Evie sat the book down and picked up the teapot. She poured him a measure but didn't fill the cup. She picked up the creamer and dipped a dollop inside, adding a lemon.

She handed the cup to him and stopped. "I'm sorry, I didn't ask. Is this how ye like yer tea?" That was odd, lemon in tea. She'd never put lemon in tea.

Manix took the cup, his fingers brushing with hers. "It's exactly how I like my tea."

He took a sip as he eyed her over the top of the cup. Evie offered him the plate of sandwiches, and Manix shook his head. "Thank ye, but I'm not hungry for food."

As Manix set his teacup down, he rubbed his hand. He lifted it, examining the back. "Evie. Are ye familiar with the various mating rituals of humans?"

Evie shifted in her chair, unsure of where Manix wanted to go with this topic, but hoped he had a point other than sex.

She shook her head as Manix's eyes met hers over his hand. "So many rituals exist. So many ways a man and woman come together."

He set his hand on the table. "In some places, the woman picks a man." He grinned as he spoke, "She would invite him to her sex hunt and…enjoy him for a while. When she grew tired of him, she'd pick another until she found one who satisfied her to become her husband."

Evie huffed, "I doubt there are many men who allow or like that. A woman who sexually jumps from man to man sounds like she's not very satisfied with herself."

Manix blew a laugh. "Evie, ye do make a great point." He sat back. "Her satisfaction is key, but so is his as well."

Manix hummed and stared out over the ocean.

Evie sat forward. "What?"

He glanced back at her. "The next ritual ye will certainly not like, but it's practiced today in a remote part of the world."

Evie picked up her tea and sipped it. "Ye have already ruined my sensibilities with a loose woman. I am certain the next won't burn my ears." Loose women wanting sex; what would Manix bring up next? She hoped he hurried to his point.

Manix stared at her. "Men go to homes where they know young available women live. They break in at night and sneak into the woman's bed. If she doesn't kick him out and is there by morning, they marry."

Evie barked a laugh, imagining her da's reaction to a man sneaking into her bedroom. "Her? What about her da? I bet the man sneaking in suffers more from her da finding him there than the woman." Evie set her cup down, clattering the china, "The man would find himself beaten blue and tossed out on his ass by morning."

Manix laughed. "I imagine that would be the case

in this part of the world, aye. But what if the woman had chilled, and he warmed her?"

Manix held his hand to her, and she placed hers in his as he spoke. "Tell me, Evie, is yer bed cold? Shall I come warm it tonight?"

Evie smirked as she yanked her hand out of his. "Fortunately, yer castle is heated." Warm her bed. If that was his "Casanova pickup line," Manix needed practice on the ritual of flirting.

Manix stared at her a moment. His regard moved out to the sea. "Doubts, Evie, doubts plague even the strongest of men. That which I cannot see, I am commanded to believe."

Evie blinked. Manix just described how she felt every time she tried to capture a photo of a ghost and failed.

Her reply came easily. This burden she'd thought over much of her life. "Must one always see to believe? Is there no faith given in what another perceives?"

Manix stared at her, his eyes softened, and he sat forward. "Evie, to have faith, it is necessary that at least once in your life you doubt, as far as possible, all things." Doubt and faith. Key components in a relationship. But for her, another rose above the rest.

"Trust, Manix. Faith trusts even when plans go against human reason or experience."

They sat staring at each other for a moment. Evie stared into his dark eyes, which seemed to hold a depth of hurt and pain. What were Manix's doubts, and why did he mention them now to her?

He picked up his cup, sipped it, and set it down. "My last ritual for ye, Evie."

Evie smirked, back to the mating ritual. What was

the last one Manix would mention?

She nodded as he grinned. "In a ritual from ancient times, women were often auctioned." Ah, history. This she knew well from her ma.

Evie sat up, warming to a subject she knew. "Aye, my ma's mentioned it. The prettiest ones' fathers herded them in like cattle and sold each to the highest bidder." Evie rolled her eyes. Back then, men treated women like brood mares. At times, dating nowadays felt the same.

She started to give a quipped reply but stopped as the next part came to her mind and hit a little too close for comfort—always being the awkward one, the odd girl out.

When she found her voice, it came out softer. "But the not-so-attractive ones. Those were not only given away, but fathers bribed the bidders with jewels and coin so any man would take them."

Evie smiled at the memory of her ma telling her about it, trying to warn her off suitors. It hadn't worked. She still chased the boys. Evie glanced at her hands, fidgeting on the table. Chasing boys, but none chased her back.

Manix chuckled. "Aye, it was the beginning of the concept of a dowry." He held his hand out to her. Evie placed it in his again, unsure of what he wanted this time. His cat and mouse game confused her.

He held her hand softly, his thumb rubbing the back, sending tingles up her arm.

He caressed her for a moment and hummed. "Evie, if ye had to give a dowry, would silver or gold buy my affections?"

Evie sat forward as his other hand came to her face

as he spoke, "If ye were to find yerself needing it, would it be gems?" He leaned forward, kissing her, catching her off guard, but not in an unpleasant way.

Manix whispered into the kiss, "A magic Iona stone to tempt me to be yours?" He deepened the kiss, thrusting his tongue in, dancing with hers. She felt lightheaded and leaned into him.

Manix shifted back and stared into her eyes. "Would ye give me yer magic Iona stones, Evie, to secure my love?"

Evie pulled his Iona stone from her pocket. "I only have one. I don't think it's enough to buy anything."

Manix's eyes went to the stone, then to hers. "Evie, to have my heart, all ye have to do is ask."

"Laird Skene, ye are summoned." A servant stood behind Manix. Evie jumped, but Manix held her hand hard, keeping her in place.

Manix bent his head to the side, speaking to the servant from over his shoulder, "He can wait. I'm busy."

The man stood taller. "He insists, now."

Manix released her and stood so fast that the chair flew back. He took a deep breath, then another.

He bent, kissing Evie hard, his voice harsh as he spoke, "Hold on to yer stone, my queen. Ye never know; it may be enough to save yer soul."

****

Manix strode from the garden, turned the corner, flicked his wrist, and shifted to the master bedroom. Shadows filled the dark space, forbidden to him without invitation. The darkness grew, and the evil presence filled the room.

~She's here, where're my stones?~

Manix fisted his hands. "It will take time. I must win her trust first."

A chuckle preceded the response. *~Trust? To fuck her? Doubtful, boy. Take her and be done with it. The stones. I must gain the stones.~*

Manix growled as the one inside grew hot with anger. "I will, in time. She's to be mine, my soul mate for eternity."

~Eternity? Not if she's truly yer soul mate.~

Manix's head flashed into the form of the one inside, then back to his human form as he struggled to control his anger. "She's mine!"

He turned to the door, nearly ripping it from its hinges as he opened it.

The force from the dark soul commanded he stop. *~The stones, boy, get me the stones.~*

****

Later, Evie stood dressed in Manix's black feather gown. She had to admit it was a gorgeous dress, and with her hair styled by a maid piled on top of her head with tendrils framing her face, she did resemble a black swan.

She moved out of her room, down the hall, and at the top of the stairs, she stood stunned. People filled the great hall below, more than she'd seen earlier in the day. Certainly, this many people couldn't stay in the castle. Manix's home was large, but not this large. As her eyes roamed the room, each person's costume got more and more elaborate. There were characters like fairies, some people in historically elaborate gowns, and others as mythical characters who danced and spoke as they enjoyed the party. It was almost as if a theatrical costume department outfitted each guest.

Someone clicked a glass three times, and Manix's voice rose above the din. "Attention, attention all!" Everyone turned to him as he stood at the base of the curved staircase.

When he looked up at her, he lifted his champagne glass. "Welcome our honored guest this evening, Evie MacDougall." He drank the entire glass as the murmurs of "To Ms. MacDougall" and "Sláinte" filtered to Evie.

Manix held his hand out to her. "Come to me, Evie." She started down the stairs as the guests smiled at her. Taking the steps one at a time, in the full gown with a handsome man waiting at the bottom, his hand out to her, she felt like a princess. When he took her hand in his, he kissed the back and held it.

A young man approached and bowed before her. "Would the swan like a dance?" Music filled the room. As people proceeded to take the dance floor, Evie spotted the string quartet in the corner.

Manix handed her to the man. "A queen. Treat her well."

He nodded. "As ye wish Mi'laird." The man escorted her to the dance floor, joining the others in a slow waltz.

Evie regarded at him as they twirled "Yer name?"

He nodded. "Aster, Mi'lady."

They made another pass around the dance floor as the other dancers flitted by. She glanced away, spying Manix with a group of men, his eyes following her every move.

The music ended, and Aster bowed. Another man pushed before her and bowed. "Manix said ye wanted to dance this evening. Indulge me." Evie turned to find Manix toasting her with a grin. The music started, and her partner took her in his arms and led her in a fast, quick step she had difficulty keeping up with. Evie tried to follow him but tripped twice.

She held her hands up. "Wait, I must rest. All this jumping, ye are killing my feet." The man bowed and led her to Manix, who held two glasses of wine. She wiggled each foot as he handed her one. She took a hearty sip as she caught her breath.

Manix leaned toward her and whispered, "My swan, how are ye enjoying yerself at the ball?"

Evie joked, his play coming to mind as her feet smarted, "All this dancing, I might make a deal with the devil to become the white swan and escape."

Manix stopped and held her to him. "If someone comes to offer ye that deal, Evie, please take it." He brushed his fingers on her face as he kissed her softly. "Take it before it's too late to save yerself."

Evie stared as he backed away. His intense expression drew her to him, almost pleading with her, but for what?

He looked down and shook his head as he gripped her hand harder. When his face lifted and met hers, the evil she saw in his eyes froze her. What was wrong with him?

The music ended, and one of the men who spoke to Manix before bowed before her. "Another dance? Maybe something slower to accommodate an injured soul." He nodded to Manix, who strode to the musicians. He bent and murmured in their ears as a lone violin began a melancholy tune. He limped as he danced with her. She twisted and helped him stay steady. He seemed to stand taller and dance better. The music changed, reminding her of Manix's unicorn play as it flashed in her mind. The night of the festival, they celebrated tonight.

Evie blinked, and the man she danced with passed her into Manix's arms. He took her into a sweeping and swirling dance, and the music built in tempo. Manix and she now danced like they made love. Manix gripped her head and turned it till he kissed her full on the mouth. The music, his hands, his mouth, it all consumed her. His tongue demanded her reaction, and she could only follow. The sensations flowed over her body in waves, building to a crescendo.

Manix held her before him as he whispered, "He captured her, taking her heart and keeping it locked away, so her love was only his, forever."

Manix took her hand in his and held it tightly as he turned them to the crowd. "Everyone, Evie, my queen, my bride."

Chapter 11

Evie jerked her hand back. "Yer what?"

Manix pulled her to his side. "Now, Evie, don't make a scene. These are our guests."

Evie tried to pull away, but he held her, gripping painfully into her side. "Yer guests, not mine." She elbowed him as she stomped on his foot.

He released her as his laughter filled the room.

She ran to the front door, tripping on her gown and losing her heels. The double doors slammed shut, the sound echoing throughout the castle. When she turned, the guests faded. Streams of clouds shot to the ceiling as each person disappeared, one then another. Evie stood rooted in the spot as hundreds of people vanished one by one like smoke sucked into the ceiling.

Manix sauntered toward her, shaking his head as he slowly stalked her. "Now, Evie, is that a way to treat our guests? Ye've made them upset. They've all left." Manix waved his hands as Evie's eyes shot around her to an empty great hall.

She ran past Manix to the balcony doors, pulling on them. The glass vibrated as she shook the latch, trying to open it.

Manix's voice came from close behind her. "There is no use, Evie. Ye are truly trapped."

She turned, and he stood in the center of the room. "Ye accepted hospitality. Partook of food I offered—

slept in my castle. My capture spell is complete. Ye are here to stay, Evie, till I say so."

Evie gripped her arms around her, a chill raking her body. "Spell?"

Manix's body slid toward her, not walking, but floating fast. She tried to step back, but something held her in place, some force.

He gripped her arms. "Ye are so naïve, Evie, but I shall remedy that soon." He kissed her hard. When he pulled back, she spat in his face.

He slapped her violently and then patted her burning face. "Evie, look at what ye made me do. Ye rile my temper. That is not wise." The last came out with a growl that sounded almost animalistic.

Manix floated, circling her as his hand waved and a force wrapped around her, holding her tight, like ropes, from her shoulders to her hips. It lifted her off the floor and left her dangling in the middle of the room. The grip was so tight she almost couldn't breathe.

Who was Manix?

His face came close, his hand cupping her cheek. "Who am I, Evie?" He sneered as her eyes went wide. "Aye, my queen, I read yer mind." He kissed her softly. "I am King, Evie, King of a Fae realm."

He sighed audibly. "My castle, Tór Mór, exists not only in the human realm but also in the Fae realm. My kingdom, coexisting in both realms."

Face to face, Evie stared into his eyes. They changed, glossing over black, then swirled into red instead of the dark black/brown they normally were. The pupils morphed into slits, and when he blinked, animal eyes stared back at her.

King, he said king. Dagda was king of the good

Fae, which meant Manix was king of...

He kissed her as his mind speak filled her head. *~Aye, my queen. King of Fomoire, the evil Fae. Youngest son to Balor. Welcome to my castle.~*

He floated away and rose before her as his arms went wide. The soft buff stone of the castle rippled and shifted. The jagged edges of black rock materialized in its place as if a wave had moved through the stone. The electric lights burst one at a time in loud popping sounds, fluttering into lit candles that reflected off the stone in a fluorescent glow, making it look like obsidian rock.

Her mind raced—King of the evil Fae. His father was Balor, the bad man who kidnapped her ma, tortured her, and left her to drown on a cold rock. The Fae fable, the Stone of Doubt, was about her. He'd already read her thoughts. Manix couldn't learn all her thoughts. As she had many times with her brother, Evie closed her mind and focused inwardly.

He flew to her, *~Aw, Evie. No, don't close yer mind to me now. Ye are so powerful.~*

She felt him crawl through her mind, like fingers digging in, trying to scrape away anything he found. She couldn't let him. Dirty, she felt dirty and used. He picked at her mind, piece by piece, till she imagined herself in fragments, left scattered in the wind.

She cried out, "It's not me ye want, ye bastard. It's the stones."

The animalistic laugh came again. Manix's mind spoke, and a force demanded her answer. Well, she'd often faced her brother's powers—had built defenses against mind control. To use the power, Manix needed the person to be weak-minded, and she was far from weak-minded.

Manix floated around her. *~As I hoped. My queen is of strong will and heart.~* The growl came again. *~Good.~*

Manix flew above her. *~Ye are correct, Evie. I want the Stones of Iona, but I want it all. The Stones, the power, and ye as my bride, my queen.~*

He held his hand over her, the force of his thoughts filling her. *~Ye and I shall rule the realms together with the stones.~*

She blocked him from her mind. *~Never!~*

His mental force pushed harder, *~The Stones, Evie. Where are they?~*

She blocked him again as the force to hold him away drained her, but she held out.

He pushed farther into her mind, *~The Stones.~*

The memory flashed before she could stop it. The Stone of Hope coming free from the Divine Family Statue in the tomb in Egypt—the two pieces she'd made into one.

Manix yelled, *~The Stone of Hope!~*

The memory of her handing it to her da flashed like a movie, then disappeared.

Manix growled, *~Where, Evie, where are they?~*

As she stared up at him, tears streamed down her face. "I don't know."

Manix's mind pushed harder. The pressure pounded in her head. She screamed, and blackness overcame her.

****

Evie's limp body floated as Manix flew to her. He took her in his arms. Goddess, she was his goddess and held more power than even she knew. Her resistance made her that much more alluring. He grew hard thinking of the will it took for her to resist his mind control. Only one other being he'd met could do so—his father, Balor, the most powerful Fae to exist. He and Evie would make strong children.

He floated, carrying her up the stairs to her bedroom, placed her on the bed, and waved as her clothing disappeared. Her naked form teased his senses.

The covers flew over her.

~Stop it, boy. Focus.~

His father's spirit always came at the worst of times, *~I shall admire my bride as much as I wish.~*

Balor's laugh filled Manix's mind as he gripped the yellow teardrop stone in his pocket. The Stone of Doubt warmed in his hand, the last connection to his father's spirit from beyond any realm.

~Ye should have pushed harder, Manix. Ye are weak.~

Manix punched the door, crashing it against the wall, part of the wood splintering into bits. *~I'll not kill her.~*

Doubts filled his mind, combined with hate and greed, all coming from his father into him. Manix took control of his emotions. He gripped the magic stone again. *~My plan will work. I will chip away at her bit by bit. In the end, she and the Stones of Iona will be ours.~*

Balor chuckled, *~Either way, I will win. There's more than one prophecy, depending on who ye ask. One sees the other's end, while another sees the other's victory.~*

Manix sighed and spoke to no one, "I know. In time, father."

****

Evie's groggy head rolled over. The scent of heady musk came heavily to her. She felt so weak, both from fatigue and starvation. She shuffled, sitting up in bed feeling chilled. She glanced down, and she was naked. She wrapped the satin sheet around her. She stood and almost tumbled to the floor, if she hadn't grabbed the doorway to the bath. She flicked the light on, and her cosmetics bag was missing. She glanced around and saw that her overnight bag had vanished as well.

She ran into the bedroom, trying to open the door. As she feared, they'd locked it from the outside. As she turned, she took in the room again—no clothing, shoes, nothing for her to wear.

Last night's memories flashed in her mind. Manix, king of the evil Fae, trapped her for the Stones of Iona, which her family kept for the good Fae.

Manix's Iona stone winked in the sunlight on the bedside table. Her cell phone was missing as well. She strode there, grabbed the stone, and held it against her chest, yearning for release. Her ma had prayed over an Iona stone, so Evie now prayed as well. With all her energy, she willed herself to be free. The stone chilled in her hand. She poured more energy and fell to the floor as exhaustion overcame her.

Evie sent energy out, and it flew back, striking her. Her powers didn't work. Escape—she needed to escape.

Her eyes flew to the balcony. She ran there, only to find those doors were locked. She stood gazing at the sun rising over the ocean. The bright morning light reflected like gems dancing in the waves. She so longed to be free.

Her world tilted as energy gathered. A Fae would appear soon. She felt dizzy and nauseous all at once. She fell to her knees and dry heaved as the floor spun.

She blinked and stared at a white, wooden plank floor. She wore a black satin sleeping gown and robe over it.

"My queen, ye shouldn't be so hard on yerself. Rise, come break yer fast, Evie."

Manix's voice grated her nerves now that she knew his purpose and goal—not her affection or love, but the magic Iona stones he desired.

He tsked, "Evie, *our* goal."

She glanced up at him. His grin went wide as he offered her his hand.

She batted it away and rose to unsteady feet, backing to the other side of the gazebo. She needed to be opposite to cancel the capture spell. Accept no hospitality.

She shook as she replied, "I want nothing from ye, Manix."

"Refusing me will not change the spell, Evie. Ye shouldn't torture yerself this way." He rose and pulled out a chair for her, "Please, come eat. Ye need it."

A chill shook her hard. She wrapped the satin around her, trying to find warmth. "No."

Manix traveled before her. Heat radiated from him, and her desire to move into his arms hit her hard. She turned and shook with the effort to resist him.

A low animal-like growl came from Manix. "Ye work hard against what exists between us, Evie. Yer powers are strong, but not as strong as mine." He touched her arm, and she jolted away.

"Please, I can comfort ye." The low growl came

again as his mind speak came to her, *~The warlock within begs ye to accept him, Evie, please.~*

She stepped back and fell down the gazebo steps, landing on her back. But her eyes never left Manix. Transfixed by his eyes, by the sheer pain she saw there.

Manix floated above her, his eyes darkening and twisting into the animal shape from the night before. *~The mating ritual, Evie. It has already begun. Today, we shall see it finished.~*

Evie lay there as Manix's body grew in size, his hair growing, floating like black waves behind him. What was he? What Hell did the evil Fae have in store for her?

~First, I smelled yer scent. Musk, like mine. So intoxicating.~ Wings flew out from his back but not incandescent and clear like Aodhán's. These were batlike, black with a leather texture. The span alone was over thirty feet. As Manix rose higher, his wings flapped, blocking the sun. Clouds gathered as thunder boomed. What was once a beautiful sunny morning broke into an angry atmosphere, dark and forbidding.

~Ye shed a tear on my skin—the second step of the soul mating ritual.~ Manix's wings flapped a loud beat as he rose above her. His body grew larger.

~Intimacy, we came so close. I wanted to take ye so badly. But to have yer virginity. I shall enjoy that.~ Manix's back rippled, and black horns burst through his clothing, ripping it as scales rippled across his skin.

~The warlock within, Evie. Ye dreamed of me, of my inner soul.~ A tail shot out from him, waving in the sky.

She had dreamed of him as a warlock but in human form. When he played the warlock, he'd been so alluring, sexy. Their encounter at the festival flashed in her mind.

Manix's voice floated to her like a caress. *~Aye, our evening together. Sexy it was.~*

His tail swung around, connecting with her feet, *~Yet ye denied me, turned away from making love to me, the king of the Fomoire.~* A horn on his tail slashed her ankle open.

As burning pain shot from her foot up her leg, Evie screamed, grabbing her ankle, trying to stop the blood flow. He'd hurt her, cut her in his anger.

Manix gathered her in his arms, close to his chest. The rough scales rubbed against her soft skin like sandpaper, making her flinch. He held her tighter as her ankle throbbed and tears poured down her face.

~Ye have angered the warlock, Evie, but it's okay.~ As he landed on the ground and sat, his wings wrapped around them, forming a cocoon. Manix breathed deeply, in and out, as his chest warmed to an intense heat. With each breath, it grew hot. With his next breath, he blew on her ankle. His breath came out as white smoke, and when it encountered her bloodied ankle, the smoke turned gray, then black as the pain receded and eventually faded.

As Manix blew again, the black smoke surrounded them, smelling like foul rotted meat. Nauseated and dizzy, she almost passed out.

Manix's voice came soft in her mind as he set her down and flew above her. *~Healing ye, Evie. This is another step in the mating ritual and another power I hold. I heal ye, and ye take another step, binding yerself to me.~*

Manix twisted his shoulders, and with a flash, a

full-sized dragon floated where Manix had been.

Shock waves rocked Evie. Manix was no warlock. He was much more dangerous—a shapeshifting cursed dragon.

His square head tilted as his red eyes focused on her, *~Another step in the soul mating ritual, Evie. Ye see my dragon, the warlock within.~* A dragon. Manix was a shapeshifting dragon, like Balor's sons.

A memory of her da flashed.

He stood in the chapel and explained parts of the duty to the Iona stones to her and her brother, "I've seen them in a dream. Balor's sons, bred for evil, are shapeshifting dragons he cursed to hunt the Stones of Iona."

Her da's chuckle filled the chapel. "They thwarted him, betrayed him at his glorious time of victory. They found them, the magic Iona Stones, and gave the good stones to Dagda, the king of the good Fae. They'd captured him, their own da. The king, so evil, cursed them still. They live a lonely life of immortality, forever caught between good and evil." Manix was one of Balor's sons, cursed, not evil. The others her da told her turned to good. The truth of their souls overcame the curse. Could Manix do the same?

Manix landed before her as the movement sent a whoosh of air over her, chilling her to the bone.

She shook as he proceeded closer. *~Yer statement of love, Evie, intimacy, and yer declaration will complete the ritual and bind ye to me for all eternity.~*

His face came even with hers as his red eyes gathered tears. *~Once complete, the dragon soul mating ritual makes me mortal.~*

A tear trailed down his cheek, rippling over his

scales, *~Please, Evie. Rescue me. Save my soul from damnation.~*

****

Manix stood over her. His plea she met with fear in her eyes, denial in her heart.

His father's voice yelled in his mind, *~Must all my sons disobey me? Yer father, yer king!~*

Manix yelled back, *~She's my soul mate. Mine!~*

A tear trailed down his scaled face and landed on her leg. She jolted and scooted back. Her eyes connected with his, registering sympathy. Could she love him like he loved her? Love the warlock, the dragon inside, and the man he was?

Manix moved closer, and her hand reached out, cupping his cheek. "Manix, ye have a good heart, a kind soul. Please take me away from this place. Take me to the Fae realm."

As he read her thoughts, the Tuatha Dé Danann's Broemere Castle flashed in his mind, the blue crystal threatening him from where he stood.

His eyes went to the black obsidian stone of Tor Castle, his father's home. *~Evie, we are in the Fae realm—the Fomoire kingdom, not the Tuatha Dé Danann.~* His dragon growled and roared in her face. She thought of him, her Fae boy. His vision shifted to red. Manix dug into her mind deeper. What had she done with her Fae boy? How close were they?

She screamed and held her head as her memory came to his mind. Both of them writhing in sexual delight in a garden by a lake in the moonlight. She'd fucked him. Her Fae boy, her virginity given to that blond ass! He roared again as he reared into flight.

Evie covered her head and screamed, "Manix,

please don't hurt me!"

Balor roared, ~*Stop thinking with yer cock and get me the stones.*~

Manix's anger grew and festered inside him. She'd betrayed him, their love. She'd given herself to the good Fae and twisted his mind against his father. His father was right: find the stones.

~ *Evie, ye will give me the Stones of Iona, now.*~ He pushed into her mind. Digging, probing, tearing through her memories. Her happy childhood, her loving family. A father and mother. Her brother she was close to. Her best friend. A happy life and home. Her screams of pain as he forced his way through her mind fed his desire to hurt her as she'd hurt him.

Nothing of the stones came to him outside of the Stone of Hope in Egypt. At the edges of her mind, pushing her sanity, he saw she didn't know where the stones were. He flew close and gathered her limp body to him. She had to know more, something. He wanted to save her—needed to save her from evil, from Balor.

~*Evie, if ye do not tell me, Balor will kill ye. Please, ye are my soul mate. I only wish to save ye. Together, we will rule the realms. I, as yer king, and ye as my queen.*~

Evie groaned and opened her eyes, staring directly into his. "I'd rather die than be yer love or yer queen."

Manix held her close as pain ripped through his heart, ~*If that is yer wish, then that shall be yer destiny.*~

****

Her world tilted. She rose and fell, landing on the floor. She rolled over, and her bed was in front of her. Back in her room at Manix's castle—trapped again.

She closed her eyes and lay there for a moment. When she opened them, Aodhán's teardrop stone sat under the bed. She grabbed the gem, holding it close as tears streamed down her face. *Aodhán, hear me. Please, Aodhán, I need ye.*

Chapter 12

Evie eventually crawled into the bed and tried to sleep. But the same night, visions that plagued her before returned. Black mist shaped like monsters chased her, but it was through Manix's castle this time. Just as before, every turn she took, another black mass rose before her, blocking her way. *No way out* rang through her mind.

Once, she rose to go to the bath for a drink. When she turned on the faucets, no water came. She returned to bed defeated.

She fell in and out of consciousness, her hunger getting the best of her as acid rose in her throat, burning her mouth, and the aches of her belly. It cramped, curved in on itself, waking her more than once. She rolled over, and the sky beyond the balcony had passed dusk into night.

Her door opened, and she sat up and fell over from dizziness.

The maid set a plate and cup on the table before the dark fireplace. "Ye are to eat."

The woman strode past the manservant Evie had seen at the gazebo the day before. Was it only a day? It felt like a week.

The man shut the door, and the lock's click echoed. Evie crawled over the large bed to the other side, slid off, and fell to the floor. She crawled to the chair, climbed up, and sat before the blessed liquid and sustenance. Her thirst won out first.

She grabbed the cup and gulped the water, soft and cool on her throat. She eyed one piece of bread on the plate when she set her cup down. She tore into that, shoving it in her mouth, savoring the full feeling the bread gave when it hit her belly, only to turn to nausea.

Evie placed her head on the table and begged Aodhán to save her. The ball of energy formed from her chest. Her hand came up and cupped it as its shape fully formed. A slight glow started, flickered, then faded. She was truly alone without hope.

Evie sat back and stared out the balcony door to the darkness beyond, feeling like it consumed her. After a time of staring, a bright green glow started and quickly formed into a person's shape. Evie blinked as The Green Lady, the ghostie of Dunstaffnage Castle, floated before the balcony door.

Evie sat forward. "Hello?"

The ghost floated up and down like Maggie did when she visited. Emotions flowed over Evie, calm and reassuring. Evie's eyes moved to the ghost's face, and her expression had Evie questioning everything in existence. For the first time, The Green Lady gave Evie an expression. She smiled at her. Evie gasped. Smiling meant good.

Evie stood on shaky legs and reached for the ghost. When her hand encountered the apparition, the ghost's mouth opened, and a wail came loud. The ghost sobbed as tears poured down her cheeks. She wailed so loudly that Evie had to cover her ears to block out the sound. The sound was so loud, the emotions so intense, Evie fell to her knees.

Her door burst open, and rough hands grabbed her, hauling her up.

When she opened her eyes, she met Manix's animal-like slits. "Ye try to call yer Fae boy to ye. We cannot have this."

He dragged her from the room and down the stairs, and she tripped near the bottom. She'd have fallen if he hadn't swept her in his arms and flew to the fireplace.

He held her, waving his hand before the picture over the fireplace. A serene painting of Tor Castle faded, and gray clouds swarmed, then faded to a scene. Aodhán stood calling for her as he flicked his wrist, twirling a glowing ball of energy precisely like the one he'd given her.

Evie cried out as Manix held her tighter. "Yer Fae boy calls to ye, Evie. Why?"

Evie shook her head, and Aodhán called again. The pull on her chest started like when the ball of energy formed.

Manix growled, "What is this, Evie? A power ye hide from me?"

He held her limp form and waved his hand over her chest, pulling the sphere of energy from her body, taking more energy from her.

Manix held the glowing ball. "Well, well, well. A calling sphere. What does the Fae boy have in store for Evie? Shall we find out?"

The maid appeared beside Manix. "Ye called?"

Manix set Evie aside, whose knees gave out, leaving her lying on the floor.

Manix grabbed the maid, who cried out, but soon stopped and stared in a daze. Manix shifted the ball in his hand and pressed it into the maid's chest. As the ball faded into her chest, the maid's face morphed. Her shape melted, then swirled, and when her face became focused again, Evie stared into a mirror. The maid even wore Evie's tell-tale black shirt and jeans. The outfit came complete with her black combat boots. Her long hair sat piled in the same top bun Evie favored.

Manix laughed. "Not bad, if I should say so myself." He waved, and the woman floated into the clouds over the fireplace. "Go to him. Let us watch and see what yer Fae boy wants, Evie."

The woman floated, disappeared, then stood next to Aodhán.

Manix picked Evie up and held her to his side. "Come, my queen, let us watch the show."

****

Aodhán sensed the air shift. The power of another coming into his realm alerted him. Evie arrived. When he turned, she stood staring at him.

He advanced quickly to her, sweeping her in his arms. "Evie, I've called for days. Ye only answered once, and it was so weak."

He held her at arm's length, "Is everything okay?"

Evie nodded and bent her head into his embrace. He held her tighter, knowing they'd not need the energy spheres to call one another again after today. He'd be in her arms for a lifetime soon enough. Aodhán shifted them to the Moon Garden, where they'd made love, the cliff over the waterfall within the moonlight—the perfect place to declare his everlasting love to her.

Aodhán held his immortality necklace to his chest. This was it. His time was upon him and so fast. Evie would accept his gift, and they would live out a lifetime together.

He stepped back, released her, and bent on one knee, "Evie. As a Fae, we do not take vows of matrimony. Here to pledge our love, it is eternal, everlasting."

Evie stood staring at him as a slight smile crossed her face. Soon, he'd see a wide laughing grin, one he would cherish for all time.

Aodhán held his necklace out to Evie. "Evie, I give ye the gift of my immortality. A pledge to live a lifetime with ye in yer realm as a mortal." He took a deep breath. "To take my token means ye bind yerself to me for all eternity, in this life and the next."

Evie beamed, and the love Aodhán felt for her flowed.

He took a deep breath and spoke the vow to give her his immortality, "Forever, my soul is kept in this stone. A part of my blood, a part of my bone. A piece of myself I give to thee. A part of my soul for all eternity."

He glanced at her. "Please take it."

Evie fingered the necklace, then took it gingerly from his hand. She backed away as she gripped it to her chest.

Wind and energy gathered around them. The light clouds of the night turned to darkness, and thunder boomed in the distance.

Aodhán stood and turned as evil energy flowed through the kingdom. This wasn't right. A cackling came from behind him. He turned and came face to face with an older woman who stood where Evie was.

She held his necklace, and her voice wasn't that of a woman but a man's. "Foolish boy, ye tempt fate this way. Mock destiny."

That voice, he'd recognize it anywhere. He'd heard

it arguing in the Fae council meetings.

"Manix!"

A bolt of light flew into the woman, causing her arms to fling out as the energy lifted her off the ground. His necklace burst into flames and disappeared from her hand. She flew into the clouds, disappearing.

Manix's laugh filled the once-serene garden. "Aodhán, prince of the Tuatha Dé Danann, the future king. Ye gave yer vow to the wrong woman. Ye failed, and it cost ye yer mortality." Anger surged in Aodhán. The woman—obviously a changeling spell. Tricked, but by whom? Evie or Manix?

Manix's whisper came to him, "Her or me? Good question. Come, Fae boy, search for yer human girl." A breath tickled his ear. "In the end, I'll have it all. The magic Iona stones, control over all the realms, and her, by my side." He huffed, "She's feisty. Good in bed. Her resistance will only kill her in the end. Hurry and see if ye can save her."

Aodhán reached out with his powers, trying to search the realms, but he came against nothing. He tried again, and nothing.

Manix's hiss came back, "Trouble there? Guess ye lost part of yer powers when ye lost yer immortality. Good luck, Fae boy."

Thunder rumbled, and the black clouds blew away, leaving Aodhán bathed in moonlight by the waterfall alone. He tilted his head back and yelled till his breath ran out. He yelled again and again till his throat hurt and his voice went raspy. A feeling he'd never felt before. Pain and helplessness. All his yelling, yet none heard him.

When he lifted his eyes, he sat alone in a meadow

in the human realm.

****

Evie sat on the floor before the fireplace, stunned as tears rolled down her cheeks. Aodhán had given his heart, soul, and immortality, and she'd been unable to take it. When he offered his necklace, she'd reached out to take it, and the woman who looked like her had. Her heart lay in pieces as she stared at Aodhán's image, his tears falling down his face like hers.

Manix turned as the clouds above the fireplace faded, and the painting of his castle appeared again. "Well, I didn't expect that outcome. That went well."

He turned, dusting his hands, and stopped when his eyes landed on her. "Aw, Evie, no tears."

He slid to her, using his Fae force, and swept her in his arms. "Come, Evie. I gave ye the chance once." He waved a hand over her head, and the hunger receded, the dizziness faded, and her body started to restore itself.

Manix brushed his lips over hers. "Be my queen, lover, and I'll make all the pain disappear."

She stared into his eyes, the slit of the animal still there.

Yet, as his power traveled through her, she detected hesitancy. "Manix, please take me away from here. Take me home. There is good in ye."

In her mind's eye, she pictured Dunstaffnage Castle, her home. A tear escaped, and she only wanted to be with her family. Her heart longed not to hurt anymore. Within it, Aodhán's voice came to her, calling her. Her love.

Manix dropped her, and the pain and hunger returned. "He calls ye, and ye long to reply."

He stormed away, stopped, and turned. "Yer Fae boy is mortal now. Will die by my hand as the fates foretold in an epic battle between the greatest Fae forces, good and evil. Our prophecy comes true—yet only one will prevail."

Manix stood taller, "This is, only if yer Fae boy can find ye—or even me."

He moved his hands in a circular motion. One undulating over the other as black clouds gathered and spun in the great room. The clouds built, consuming the room, Evie, and the castle. The world tilted, then twirled. As Manix's laugh echoed, the earth twisted feeling as if she traveled through a portal. Evie sensed Manix knew what he was about. He shifted the entire castle in space and time, but to where Evie had no clue.

Chapter 13

Aodhán gazed around him at the beauty of the meadow. Vast mountains rose behind a serene lake with a waterfall. He sat on a hillside, the green grass itching his arm. A cold breeze blew. He shivered from the cold for the first time. A cloud moved, and the sun's rays hit him, warming him. He took a deep breath as something tickled his nose. He sneezed and took a breath. Halfway in, he sneezed again. He chuckled—mortality and its rewards. His eyes went to the sky. He had imagined sharing this moment with Evie, but that wasn't the case.

He twisted his wrist, bringing forth the calling sphere. Nothing happened. No warming occurred in his heart; no energy gathered in his soul.

Where had his powers gone? Butterflies tickled his belly. He glanced down, almost expecting to find a couple. There was none, just a sensation.

He sat on his knees, focused, and called the sphere to him again—Nothing. He stood and raised his right arm to the sky, calling for the energy of the realms, his Fae energy, and a spark flew from his finger.

He sat hard. Well, this must be the price of changing fate, the cost of his Fae powers. Aodhán glanced around again, noting the meadow resembled the Moon Garden in the Fae realm. Then it hit him; everything co-existed from the Fae realm to the human realm. It was why they were so dependent on one another. A rule the humans had forgotten from long ago but to a Fae, not overlooked.

His eyes traveled the mountain range, and soon it clicked. He sat on the back side of Ben Chruachan. Dunstaffnage Castle was a hike through the pass. If he found his way to the chapel portal, where Fae energy gathered, maybe what little powers he had left would take him to the Fae realm, home to Broemere Castle.

Manix was after only one thing: the magic Iona Stones. He'd use Evie, this Aodhán knew. He feared Evie would hold out, keeping the stones secret till her life force had nothing left. He had to find Manix, get to Evie, and save her before nothing was left to save.

He stood resolved to do this as a mortal. He'd have to hike the pass and make his way into the Dunstaffnage area and the chapel while surviving as a mortal man—a test for any man who'd lived only with Fae abilities. He could survive if he approached like Evie's ancestors, men who lived off the land. He took off on foot, wishing for a plaid, a broadsword, flint, and a handful of oats, a highlander's essentials. Keeping his eye on Ben Chruachan, he kept the list running in his mind.

****

After hours of hiking, as he crested the first ridge, he came upon a horse tied to a tree. Aodhán pulled up short, not trusting the answer to his prayers that stood before him. The all-white stallion carried a fully loaded saddle. A broad sword, shield, and full saddlebags hung on the side.

Aodhán spoke lowly as he neared the animal, "Are ye an evil Fae come to trick me in the human realm? Maybe a will-o'-wisp come to give me help in my time of need?"

The horse turned to him and winked as Brigid's voice entered his mind. *~Take what gifts I offer, son. And don't make a fuss. The Fae Council will call me out for meddling where I ought not to.~*

Aodhán chuckled as he approached the fine animal. *~Thanks, Ma, but ye couldn't have sent some Fae powers, a magic stone? Maybe even a car?~*

The horse whinnied in response.

Aodhán stood smirking. "Guess I shall call ye Willow then." He patted his neck as he took the reins, mounted as the animal shied, and took off at a gallop for the pass.

After hours of rotating a run to a walk to not tire Willow, Aodhán slowed at a stream. He dismounted and let the reins go so the animal might quench his thirst. Aodhán bent beside the fine creature, cupping his hands and gulping the cold water. He stood, retrieved the empty water pouch he'd sipped from off and on, and filled it at the stream before returning it to the saddle. He patted Willow as he grabbed the reins and led him to the shade of a tree, tying him there for a rest. Willow eyed him for a moment, then bent, pulling tufts of grass with his teeth, munching contently.

Aodhán sat against the tree, allowing its branches to shade him, hoping for a short rest. His rush to get to Evie had him in knots, but a human's progress across open land had him at a disadvantage. He cursed himself and his blind naivety for plowing headlong into giving his immortality without thinking it through. Now, he sat in the human realm, unable to shift in a moment to save Evie.

He took a deep breath. Evie was a smart girl, a

strong woman. She had to hold out. He smirked. Manix had to keep her alive and well. She was his bait.

Disgust rolled over his body and twisted through his soul. Evie was Manix's toy, and he played with her in his search for the stones to take control of both realms. Now that Manix knew Aodhán gave and lost his immortality, the game's stakes rose, and Manix's perverse enjoyment of it increased. He huffed. Hell, Manix may be the reason Aodhán landed in the human realm. Either way, Aodhán would see to Manix's end as foretold.

Aodhán sat and thought for a moment. What drove Manix on the same quest as his father? Balor died only recently, and Manix took the throne. Why come after the stones so quickly? Balor had only announced Manix's existence just before his death—claimed him to be his long-lost son.

Willow shied and yanked on his reins, grunting with the effort to escape an unseen foe. Aodhán stood and flung his hand out, twisting the wrist, calling for a spell. Nothing happened. He cursed himself. *No Fae powers, idiot.* Mortality would take some getting used to.

He moved to the horse who still fought the tied reins and struggled to pull the broad sword from the scabbard attached to the saddle. When he finally freed it and turned, he found what spooked the horse. A wild boar stood not but a few feet from Aodhán.

Aodhán easily gripped the blade's handle, calling upon his work in confinement. He stepped to the right to get closer to the boar's flank. The animal grunted and shifted, preparing for a charge. Aodhán bent his knees and held his sword at the ready. Once thrust through the throat, up into the head, it would end this easily. He waited for the boar's first move.

In a squeal, the boar charged. As the animal jumped, Aodhán crouched down. As the animal came at him, Aodhán came under his body and gained the leverage needed to thrust his sword from its throat through to its head, killing him instantly.

The boar's weight came on him, and Aodhán rolled to the side, twisting his blade, ensuring the animal had died.

He lay there panting, not believing he'd just taken a life. The good Fae regarded life with honor and respect in the Fae realm. Only evil Fae took life needlessly. Well, Aodhán supposed this wasn't needless; it was in defense. He stood, placed his foot on the boar's head, and pulled the blade free with a sucking sound, leaving blood gushing from the wound. He bent over, nauseous. Well, the human realm certainly had its doses of reality.

On instinct alone, he pulled the boar aside and began the arduous task of gutting and butchering the animal—no use leaving good meat for the crows.

Hours later, he had portions of meat wrapped and stored on the back of Willow, and he glanced up. The sky cast hues of orange and red that faded into purple near the mountains. Dusk had settled over the human realm. He wasted half a day without travel but had meat and a newfound pride. He survived in the human realm without magic. He chuckled. Go figure, a Fae prince living as a human, hunting and butchering his meat.

Aodhán set up camp quickly as the light faded fast in the mountains, and the chill overcame him fast.

He flicked his wrist to spark the campfire. When

nothing happened, Willow nickered.

Aodhán turned, replying as if the horse understood him, "Yea, yea, yea. No Fae powers. Use the flint, idiot."

He retrieved the flint and knelt, striking the plate. Again and again and again. When he'd about lost hope and the feeling in his cold hands, a spark flashed, and a flame caught. He yelped and quickly fed his fire. Soon, he had a blazing fire and meat on a stick roasting. He leaned against the tree, congratulating his work, wondering if this was what the Fae Trials were like. A journey of rights from youth into adulthood where a Fae father took his son into the roughest parts of the realm to test their Fae abilities and declare them men.

A burning smell floated, and he jerked his meat from the fire. Poking his finger at the burnt meat, he figured the meal wasn't a total loss. He sat back and took a bite, noting its tough texture. What he wouldn't give for one of the Fae's fine meals now.

A trial that declared him a man. A bitterness settled in him. The Tuatha Dé Danann stopped the ritual after the Fomoire laid siege to a party and massacred the group, sparking the first of the Fae wars for the Stones of Iona.

He took another bite of his meat, chewed, and washed the rough morsel with cool river water. The wars, his father's battle and death—it settled in his heart much like his meal settled now, hard like a rock.

He wished he'd been able to do the trial with his father. Asmund, his father, died in a battle in Aodhán's youth. He recalled the many talks his father had with him about Balor, the evil Fae. Telling him how Dagda, his grandfather, believed evil thoughts came to a man's mind when evil resided inside his soul.

Asmund felt differently.

His father explained that to understand evil, one must know evil. Knowing and understanding evil didn't make one evil, only more powerful. Capable of taking down one's foe. Bitterness wrapped itself around the rock in Aodhán's belly. The dream his father's spirit showed him shortly after his death came to his mind now. The Fae battle, brutal and fierce, spell after spell, rocked each side's forcefield. His father, spotting a weakening Fomoire Fae, Balor, shot a spell through an opening in the forcefield. Sensing the oncoming spell, Balor shifted his wife before him, blocking the spell. She, unaware, took on the full force of the spell and died.

Asmund had stood in shock. He'd not intended to take another's life, but he had. In Balor's rage, as his wife lay dead in his arms, he wiped the entire contingent of Tuatha Dé Danann out in one powerful spell outlawed by the Fae council. Everyone, including Balor's fighting force, died that day. Only his two dragon-shapeshifting sons, Dameon and Tiberius, survived with him. At first, Balor rejoiced, since the magic Iona stones had saved his sons' lives. The magic stones he thought were now in his possession. His sons had betrayed his trust, captured him, and turned him and the gems over to Aodhán's grandfather, king of the Tuatha Dé Danann. Evil turned to good.

Aodhán called out his father's spirit. He hadn't heard from him since his death, his soul at rest. But right now, he could use his support and advice. He reached out with his Fae power, his soul.

Nothing came back, only the stillness of the night.

He tossed the stick into the flames and settled against the tree, hoping rest came easily to him. As he tried to relax, his mind churned. Evie, what must she be thinking? He concentrated on her, her soul, her life force. With his Fae powers, he'd sense her anywhere, but without, he had only echoes left from memory. But the memories were a welcome relief. He drifted off to images of them in the moon garden in his mind. Sleep washed over him, and the dream shifted to the Fae realm. He battled against a foe, one powerful and swift. Spell after spell, he cast but missed each time. The Fae eluded him. No matter how hard he tried, he failed each time.

Evie floated before him, begging as she cried. Her face morphed into the Green Lady of Dunstaffnage, who cried. The spirit, familiar to him, a former Lady MacDougall from the past who never let go, hovering in the human realm, watching over the family, warning of fates yet to come. Crying meant bad, and smiling meant good. Today, she cried, begging him to help Evie find her. But it was Evie's voice he heard. The torment in her plea tore his heart, ripping at his soul. He tried to reach her. He tried to find her like before, with his feelings, but he failed. Her voice stopped. The silence was deafening. He sat up with a yell as Willow jolted. The early rays of dawn greeted him.

He stood and shook himself. Evie called for him and begged for rescue. His powers must not be totally gone. He kicked dirt over the coals, then rummaged through the saddle bags, finding an oat cake. He mounted Willow and shoved the whole dried cake into his mouth. He needed to move. Evie needed him. Mortal or not, he had to save her.

Chapter 14

Aodhán galloped into the meadow. The paved road to Dunstaffnage marked a route to his destination. The sun crested the mountain range as a new day dawned. Only one day of travel felt like an eternity to Aodhán, who bent time and shifted to his destination. He pushed Willow, hoping the stallion didn't mind, and the horse answered with a nod and faster pace, sensing his rider's desperation.

Aodhán burst through the tree line beside Loch Etive and raced across the castle yard without caring who had spotted him. When he came upon the Chapel in the Woods, energy gathered and swirled. Someone used the portal. Based on the energy collected, they used it for something large.

Willow reared as the wind whirled and the portal gaped wide. A large eighteenth-century galleon ship popped out of the portal, landing in the loch by the dock beyond the castle.

Aodhán calmed his horse as he stared in disbelief. A whole ship traveled the portal. It took immense power to achieve such a feat. Was it an evil Fae he would face this day?

Male laughter came from inside the small holy building as Ewan MacDougall stumbled out the door, followed by Doug MacArthur, dressed in pirate garb from the eighteenth century.

Ewan held his stomach as he folded over. "Did ye see his face when we took his gold then disappeared, ship, crew and all?"

Doug clapped him on the shoulder. "Aye, and the lassie who only had eyes for ye. She was a buxom lass if I ever saw one!"

Aodhán sat on his horse, frozen. Evie's brother and best friend walked toward him. Willow shifted and nickered, bringing both men up short as Ewan drew his sword.

Aodhán sat still, waiting to see what both would do, faced with a strange man who looked more Fae than human.

It was Ewan who moved first.

He stepped forward, lowering his weapon. "It's ye, isn't it? Evie's Fae boy?"

Aodhán dismounted and came forward. "Aye, it is I, Aodhán."

Doug came up beside Ewan. "I'll be damned. He looks just like Brigid."

Aodhán rubbed his neck. "Of course I do. I'm her son. But I don't have time for chatter. Evie. She's in danger, and I need yer help."

Ewan sheathed his sword. "I knew it! The fable is about her!" He came to Aodhán, fists raised. "If ye have harmed my sister…"

Aodhán threw up his hands, emitting a force field out of instinct, and it held, knocking Ewan on his rear end.

He held it there, thankful some Fae powers had returned. "It's not me who has Evie. It's the king of the Fomoire Fae, the evil Fae."

He released the field, stepping forward and

offering his hand to help Ewan up.

Ewan took it as Aodhán spoke, "I need yer help getting back to the Fae realm. I must find her."

Ewan nodded, "Then let's go."

Larid Colin MacDougall, Ewan's da, called from the castle yard, "Ewan, damn ye! I saw the ship come through the portal. What are ye boys up to now?"

Ewan's eyes went wide as Doug grabbed him. "Shit, Ewan, yer da. He saw the ship fly from the portal. He'll tan our hides for sure!"

Aodhán jerked them toward the chapel. "I don't have time for this. Open the portal, hold it till I get through, close it, and keep yer da from finding out."

As he pulled them along, Ewan and Doug tripped after him.

Ewan lifted his hands toward the chapel doors and then paused as he turned his face to Aodhán. "Ye will save my sister. She loves ye, and ye will save her. Promise me."

Aodhán nodded. "I love her with all my soul from now to eternity. I will save her."

Ewan waved his hands, and the door spun as the Broemere throne room came into focus. Aodhán jogged through and turned to wave to Ewan.

Colin came up behind Ewan and Doug. "Why do ye have the portal open?"

Ewan smirked as Doug turned and replied, "Practicing his Fae powers, Laird Mac, nothing more."

The portal swirled, and the human world faded.

Aodhán took a deep breath and then another.

Finally, back in the Fae realm, he heaved a sigh of relief as a familiar voice boomed across the room, "About time ye showed yer happy rear end up, grandson. There's a lot ye must answer for."

Aodhán's shoulders crept to his ears at his grandda's tone. He must face his king for his actions—tempting fate and failing so miserably. Last time, it was eight human years in Fae prison. He prayed this time it wouldn't be so long; Evie couldn't hold out.

He lowered his shoulders as his father's voice echoed in his memory, "Face yer fate and overcome yer fear, then ye will always prevail."

He stood taller, feeling more like a man now than ever before.

Aodhán turned and faced his grandfather, his king. With a bow he spoke, "Aye, I am back and ready to face my fate, but first, we must find Evie."

Dagda barked a laugh. "Evie? Hell, boy, ye tempt fate, and all the realms fall into chaos. Evie missing is the least of our worries."

Aodhán stood still, staring at his grandda, mentor, his king.

Dagda growled as he stood slowly.

His fists clenched, and his knuckles popped. "Ye try to cheat destiny. Gave yer immortality to the wrong woman who wasn't yer soul mate, casting it into the unknown."

He stepped from his throne toward Aodhán. Aodhán usually shook when his grandda did that, but not this time. He stood tall and faced his king. Evie needed him.

Dagda grunted as he took a step toward him. "Yer soul mate is now bait, meant to draw ye into the prophecy. A weakness to use against ye, against us."

Dagda stopped before him and folded his massive arms. "But that's still not the worst we face."

Aodhán stood staring into his grandda's eyes as Dagda blocked his mind from him. What did they face now?

Dagda started in a whisper that grew into a yell by the end, "Just when I need the one Fae who has the powers to battle the evil Fae, the Fomoire king, ye lose most yer powers to a lost promise. The realms need ye! I need ye!"

Aodhán stood still, refusing to flinch. "What has happened?"

His mother, Brigid, moved behind his grandda. "The Fomoire. They have gone."

Aodhán glanced between the two. "Gone? Have they fled?"

Dagda barked a laugh and turned fast, returning to his throne, sitting hard. "No, disappeared. The whole damn realm. Millions cry for help at once, altering me, then silence."

He sat forward and pointed a finger at Aodhán. "And the one Fae powerful enough to find them has lost most of his powers."

Aodhán stepped back. Gone, disappeared. The whole realm? All those Fae, millions, taken to God knew where. He reached out, and his powers flickered. He reached out again, and they sparked inside, then faded. His eyes connected with his grandda, his king.

Dagda stared back, his voice grave. "Ye can't find them, can ye, son?"

Aodhán gripped his head as he screamed, "No!" He paced. "I'll find them, I promise."

Dagda pounded his throne arm. "Bah, I've given ye too much. Ye have lived all yer life with the greatest Fae powers, and ye grew complacent, which fed yer naivety."

Aodhán fisted his hands. "I will, grandda. I just need to find the way."

Dagda barked a laugh. "How, son? Ye lost most yer powers."

Aodhán stopped and faced his relative, his king. "True love. Manix sits in the Fomoire kingdom. Manix has Evie. I find Evie; I find the missing kingdom. I found her once in the realms. I'll find her again."

His grandda smiled wide. "That's the way, son."

Aodhán's gaze met his grandda's. "Ye knew the answer all along. Why didn't ye tell me?"

Dagda chuckled. "Lessons are learned better the hard way."

His grandda pointed his finger at him. "That is why ye must work, search for yer love. If ye must work for the things ye desire, the rewards are that much sweeter."

Aodhán focused on the realms, searching for his way. He felt a tingling, a notion of another there. The gods, they sent a signal. Was it really so simple?

Aodhán sensed his powers grow, the force of the realms returning his call. He strode to the window overlooking the Broemere Ocean—the cliff overlooking the Tuatha Dé Danann realm—one of the most sacred and powerful places in the realms. He lowered his head as he called upon the gods to come to him. He held his arms out as they answered his call one by one, giving him vitality and power.

His grandda growled from his seat, "Son, ye call upon the gods? They will not answer. Ye are not king."

At first, it was a tingling, then an awareness. One powerful and mighty came to his summons.

He breathed, "The gods, they come." They came in force, not in body, and the group emerged into his mind, ready to fill his soul.

Óðinn came forward first. The ruler of the gods. God of war, associated with wisdom, poetry, and magic.

Aodhán begged for his powers and for help to save his love. Implored to the gods to see him through this challenge.

Óðinn filled him with energy, fortifying him, making him stronger.

Thor, son of Óðinn, god of thunder and battle, and his wife Sif came, giving a part of their gifts.

Sif uttered, "Find yer true love, Aodhán. She needs ye."

Magni, son of Thor, god of strength. Eir, the goddess of healing. Vör, the goddess of wisdom. Each one gifted him with their powers. More came. More gave to him, feeding his Fae soul, restoring powers lost in a promise gone amiss. Each filled his heart and gave him hope and faith—removing all doubts.

Sjöfn, the goddess of love, came to him. Evie's call pierced through, painful and waning.

Aodhán raised his arms to the skies and implored upon all the gods, *I must find her*. Lightning struck him, coursing through his body, igniting a strong force he'd never felt before.

Evie's call came again. He felt it and identified its power but couldn't lock on it. Evie needed him. She called him, and he would heed her plea. The gods faded, and the energy remained inside him, pulsing in its newfound power. He lowered his arms as he lowered his head. The gods gifted him his powers again, the same yet stronger. His heart beat a steady rhythm. His breath huffed in exertion, reminding him he was still mortal—Fae and powerful, yet mortal.

He lifted his face to his king. "Through Evie, I'll find them. Then I'll battle the evil king, as foretold. I'll win, my king."

Dagda sat back on his throne, grinning wide. " 'There is a sacredness in tears. They are not the mark of weakness but of power. The power of tears shall quell any person.' "

Aodhán whispered, "The fable of the Stone of Doubt. Ye quote it."

Dagda nodded. "Aye, Manix must have the magic stone. It is the only powerful thing to make an entire realm disappear."

Aodhán bowed. "I'll get the stone."

"Aye, ye may win, but can ye save the woman as well?"

Aodhán beamed at his grandda, recalling the quote from the Fae fable story, " 'But let him ask in faith, with no doubting. For the one who doubts is like a wave of the sea that is driven and tossed by the wind.' No doubts; only through my love will I prevail."

Dagda chuckled. "Well, grandson, ye might make a great Fae King one day."

Brigid sighed. "Thank the gods Da's not mad I sent a unicorn to the human realm."

Aodhán turned to his mother. "Willow is a unicorn?"

Dagda growled, "Daughter, I shall deal with yer meddling later." He turned to Aodhán. "Time to meet yer fate, Aodhán. Ye must face this duty on yer own. Time to fight the king of the evil Fae."

****

Evie lay on her side, back on the floor of her room, exhaustion overwhelming her body, but her mind stayed focused.

Aodhán. He must find her, must come for her. She'd hid his tear-drop stone under the bed. She gripped it now but had to be careful how she called to him. It must be a way Manix couldn't sense.

She lay there a moment, resting then a moment more, allowing her mind to float. Memories of playing with her brother, Ewan, came to her. As teens, they'd tested their mental connection. It waned at a kilometer.

Once, she'd connected with an animal, a dog, casting her mind to the animal, then on to Ewan. He claimed, at first, he'd not known it was her, hidden in the animal. He didn't recognize her till she said something; only both knew. They'd steal rowies from Mrs. A without her knowing and blame their da.

As youths, the powers frightened them. As time went on, they grew used to them and tested the boundaries. Because of this, they'd made their first promise over the powers, "always look out for one another and help each other without question." Later, they'd soon learned their powers came from within and weren't a gift as Brigid claimed. Something more powerful than they'd ever dreamed.

A signal to Aodhán. Cast onto another, lengthen the signal, hoping to reach her brother or Aodhán. But who to hide within? She cast her power out, careful to mask it from Manix. She found him brooding in his study downstairs, drinking the day away as his powers peaked and faded. Whatever he was up to seemed to take all his energy and focus. Good. This was her chance.

Her energy faded as weakness overtook her, but she swallowed the bile in her throat and focused as she gripped the tear gem. There had to be a soul nearby that she could borrow, someone or some being that could help. Farm animals beyond Manix's property flashed in her mind. No, not strong enough. She needed something almost mystical—like Manix's unicorn tale.

The unicorn in the Fae realm, could she reach him?

She tried again and couldn't find him. She tried again and couldn't get any farther than Tor Island. Overcome with fatigue, she became dizzy and seemed to doze.

In her dream, the white unicorn came to her, bowed his head, and nuzzled her hand. She cast herself into him, sending a message to Ewan through him. The unicorn stepped back, breaking contact and causing her to fall forward to the ground. Weak, she lay there and thought of Aodhán, wishing to be with her love. The unicorn nudged her hand again, then curled around her, protecting her. She rested her head on his neck, petting his cheek, thankful for his comfort as her awareness faded.

Chapter 15

Fae energy pulsed inside him. Aodhán reveled at the feeling of magic forces within him again. He took a deep breath and let it out. Now fortified, he felt armed and ready. *Focus on Evie.* Finding Evie in the realms, the known, was one feat, but locating her in the unknown, a place Manix purposely hid her, himself, and an entire kingdom. Well, that would take the effort his grandda teased at being hard work and much more.

Aodhán stopped and thought about shifting to the moon garden. Would his powers amplify from the echoes of his and Evie's lovemaking?

Dagda's voice boomed in the throne room, "Focus with yer powers, son, not yer emotions."

Aodhán turned back, yelling, "It is our emotions that power the stones. Our love binds us across space and time!"

Dagda grunted, "Aye, yer love, not yer sex."

Aodhán turned toward his grandda. "I cannot focus if ye keep interrupting. Didn't ye say I had to do this alone?"

Dagda stood and bowed. "Aye, that I did. The Broemere cliff, son. It's the most powerful of all places in the Fae realm." His grandda turned, walking away.

When his mother, Brigid, didn't follow, his grandda stopped. "Come, daughter, leave yer son to his destiny."

His mother stood still, staring. A tear escaped and trailed down her cheek. She came to him slowly.

Her sad gaze stayed on him. "Take care, my son. I love ye and shall pray to the gods for yer success." She kissed his cheek, then stepped back, patting it like when he was a little boy. When she turned and followed his grandda, he sensed it was the last time he'd see her, like this, as her son.

Aodhán shook himself. He needed to focus. Concentrate on Evie. Find Evie, and he'd find the Fomoire and Manix. Through Manix, he'd find the Stone of Doubt and Evie. He prayed he had enough of everything for both tasks.

He sat at the edge of the throne room over the cliff, leaving him near floating. He'd levitate if he had the energy to spare. The weightlessness would help his focus, but he needed all his Fae power to find Evie and battle Manix. He knew the battle would be fierce. Manix would likely not follow Fae law as his father Balor had many times before. But Aodhán was ready. His mother said that to understand evil, one has to have evil inside them. Before his death, his father said just understanding it—its source was enough.

His voice rang in his memory, "Ye can still be good and know evil. Understand its source, and ye can beat that."

His mind drifted. Manix's source of evil. Greed, jealousy? No, it was something more complex. Focus on Evie, her heart, her soul, her love. As he reached out to her, the familiar feeling of her aura filled his mind, the sensations he felt when he'd first found her in the Eye of Ra so many years ago.

He cast his feelings into the realms, searching for

her, repeatedly in all the known places. After a time, nothing. He focused harder and centered more on Evie, all he knew of her. He started in the human realm. He began with Tor Island, the human location of the Fomoire kingdom, Balor's castle there, well, Manix's now. It sat empty, void of all life. Well, Manix wouldn't make his search that easy.

Aodhán refocused. He focused on Evie's aura and mentally searched each kingdom in the Fae realm. One by one, she wasn't there. Some of Fae's feelings came to him, some sharp, others faint. A general sense of worry for the Fomoire kingdom, now missing. His focus had waned and wandered, worried about his fellow Fae.

Stop, ye must stay on Evie.

Transported to Tor Island, in the human realm, he hoped Manix had forgotten, maybe left a clue. All the buildings had vanished. Only the land remained void of life—no livestock, fish, and mammals, but plants lived and thrived. The wind blew, water flowed, and the sun shone. Mother Earth was present, but nothing else.

As he turned one way and another, the wind shifted, and energy gathered. Fae energy gathered, weak. An undercurrent wafted over him. He stood ready for what would come—maybe Manix?

Horse hoofs galloped in the distance. A steady beat of the running animal thundered in his head. The closer it came, the rhythm pulsed in his heart. What would come in the form of a horse?

The drumming came close, and Aodhán's heart was about to burst. A white unicorn burst through the tree line where the castle had stood. The animal stopped and heaved his chest as he breathed in gulps of air as if he'd run a great distance. Aodhán stood, waiting, but for what, he had no clue. The only time he'd encountered a unicorn was with Evie. He cocked his head and reached out with his emotions. Was this Evie's unicorn?

He stepped forward. "Is that ye? A will-o'-wisp come to give me help in my time of need?"

The unicorn nodded and pawed at the grass.

Aodhán crept closer, not sensing any evil from the stallion, only desperation. The closer Aodhán came, the more and more the mammal resembled Willow, the horse his ma sent to him in the human realm.

When he came close enough, he held his hand out. "Willow, is that ye?"

The unicorn nuzzled his hand, and Evie's presence washed over him.

He gasped. "Evie?"

Her voice shot into his mind, then wavered as it spoke, as if distorted from traveling so far, ~*I'm here, Aodhán. Please come. I'm here.*~

He wanted to yell but didn't, fearing he'd startle the unicorn. He spoke lowly back, "Where? I cannot see."

Her response wavered and was so faint he almost didn't hear it. ~*Must one always see to believe? Is there no faith given in what another perceives?*~

His response to his grandda came to his mind, the Fae fable quote. " 'But let him ask in faith, with no doubting. For the one who doubts is like a wave of the sea that is driven and tossed by the wind.' No doubts, only through my love will I prevail."

He touched the unicorn's cheek. "Where, Evie, where?"

Her reply blew through the wind, *~Fomoire Castle.~*

The unicorn reared and fled.

Aodhán yelled after the animal, "Where? I cannot see!"

Her earlier reply echoed in his mind, "Must one always see to believe? Is there no faith given in what another perceives?"

I must see what I don't. I must have faith in Evie. He turned, taking in the cliffside where Fomoire Castle once stood.

He murmured as he focused his energy, "It's here. I must believe to see. No doubts. Only through my love will I prevail."

Aodhán poured all his energy into concentrating on Evie. She was here; he only had to believe. His love, care, and devotion all wrapped into one as he focused. Her sob came through, then her sigh. He sensed her soul. She was here!

He opened his eyes and stood at Fomoire castle, clear as day before him. It wavered like a candle flame and then showed brightly in the sunlight. The voices of millions of Fomoire trapped and angry came hard and loud to Aodhán. Each cried for help all at once in a burst of energy.

Cloaked—the kingdom Manix had cloaked! How could Aodhán be so forgetful? Balor's sons were all shapeshifting dragons possessing the power to cloak themselves and other objects. The energy needed to cloak an entire kingdom was vast. Manix had to have the Stone of Doubt. Aodhán would see it to the guardian of the stones to join with the others.

Manix's mind speak came to him, slithering into

his mind like the snake Manix was. *~Hello, Aodhán. Welcome to my home. I'm surprised ye found it. Took ye long enough.~*

****

Evie sensed a stirring, a warmth in her soul—so tired, so drained. She curled into the unicorn's side, thankful for his presence. She tightly held Aodhán's teardrop gem stone to her chest, wishing he was with her.

She sent out another message, a call to her dream boy, now her dream man, *~I'm here, Aodhán. Please come. I'm here.~*

Something pricked her mind as Aodhán voice came softly. *~Where? I cannot see.~*

She smiled in her dream, half in and out of consciousness.

Her heart spoke. *~Must one always see to believe? Is there no faith given in what another perceives?~*

Aodhán's feelings shifted. Frustration and anger came to her: half dream, half not. Evie wasn't sure anymore. She clutched the gem, hoping to wake home safe and sound, but her dream wouldn't let go. She drifted, uncertain, like lost in the sea as doubts wavered in her mind.

Aodhán touched her cheek, *~Where? Evie, where?~*

The sensation tingled, restoring her faith. Had he found her, or was this all part of her dream?

She whispered, *~Fomoire Castle.~*

Was Aodhán here? She tried to sit up but couldn't.

Strong arms grabbed her as Manix's voice rang in her head, dripping in sarcasm. "Come, Evie. Yer knight in shining armor has arrived. Let's greet him together."

Manix dragged her from the floor and on farther—to where, she couldn't tell. She stumbled along, unable to stand. Manix held her as his mind screamed to another. Fae energy gathered in a great force, pressing in on her. Her mind went blank as the world tilted, then spun. Already dizzy, she lost focus but recognized the force. It was like shifting through the portal, but this was much larger and more forceful. Many voices cried out as one.

Pain radiated as Manix dropped her. She lay stunned.

Arguing. They argued over what, she wasn't certain.

So tired, so drained.

The unicorn returned and wrapped around Evie, giving her warmth, comfort, and a little strength.

The unicorn replied, *~Rest, my dear. Yer love fights for us all.~*

****

Aodhán took to the skies, an automatic defensive move from much practice. Suspended, he could gather energy more easily and form a shield without worrying about the ground. He flew around the stately building. Its opulence was in stark contrast to the vile one who owned it. Manix had to be here, but where? When he came around the back, his focus quickly found Manix on a second-story balcony.

Their eyes locked, focused on each other—evil and hate flowed from Manix as he tried to penetrate his mind. Aodhán had to readjust so it wouldn't invade his mind as Manix intended.

Manix laughed. *~Arrived at last. But are ye in time to save the one ye want?~* Manix reached behind him and pulled.

Evie stumbled out of the doorway and would have fallen if Manix hadn't held her, ~*Beautiful, isn't she? A bit weak from her fight...*~ Manix caressed her cheek and then kissed her full on the mouth, ~*By the end of the day, my wife, she will be.*~

Aodhán sensed his anger rise. His desire to hurt Manix overwhelmed him. But if he cast a spell in anger without focus, he might hit Evie.

Manix laughed. ~*The good Fae boy can't fight this way.*~ Manix dropped Evie's hand as he twisted his shoulders and shifted into a dragon in the blink of an eye. Aodhán had heard of Balor's sons, the dragon shapeshifters, but had never seen one in their form until today. The black dragon flew high, his scream high and piercing, painful to Aodhán's ears.

His gaze flew back to Evie, who lay on the balcony floor.

He reached out to her and sent a spell to heal. It was blocked, bouncing off.

Manix's voice spoke in Aodhán's head, ~*Oh, we can't have that. Her rescue is not in the plan.*~

With the tilt of Manix's head, the castle transformed into a black obsidian rock, like in the Fae realm. Loud crunching noises followed the stones' transformation as they changed from sand to black, each turret forming a point reaching to the sky as black clouds materialized and thunder boomed. Manix took them all to the Fae realm. Now freed of entrapment, the Fomoire Fae within sighed in relief.

One for good, two for bad. This meant Manix had full use of his powers, including a magic Iona Stone. Aodhán needed to be ready, but what about Evie?

When Aodhán glanced back to the balcony holding Evie, a cage had formed over the opening, trapping her as she lay on the floor. He desperately wanted to go to her but had to deal with Manix first.

He sent her a mind speak, ~*Please hold on, Evie.*~ No reply came.

When Aodhán's eyes turned to Manix in his dragon form, the dragon grinned. ~*Now, we shall see the end of this cursed prophecy. I shall have Evie as my queen, and ye shall be dead.*~

He'd imagined this day since his grandda first told him of the prophecy—or at least his part. The prophecy itself spanned hundreds of human years involving many. His gaze shot to Evie. He never imagined one part of the prophecy would weave into another, but it seemed it had.

Aodhán closed his eyes and sent healing energy to Evie. Not a spell; he detected the shield Manix placed over the cage preventing Aodhán from reaching her, but their minds and souls remained linked from so many years ago. He took a breath and paused a moment. Nothing came back from Evie. He prayed to the gods. *Help her, heal her.* He'd see them through this together.

Manix's growl brought his attention back to him as Aodhán flew higher, preparing for the battle upon them.

Aodhán whispered as he gathered his energy, "And now, it begins."

Chapter 16

Aodhán sensed energy gathering from Manix as he amassed his own, preparing for the first strike. The wind shifted, then blew hard. The ocean churned as the waves crashed against the cliff. The roar of the wind accentuated the beat of the sea, nearly matching the beat of Aodhán's heart. The palpable energy in the atmosphere marked the beginning of a great Fae battle. Aodhán's insides quivered. It had been a while since he'd practiced Fae war. A real battle he'd never experienced. Then again, the same was true for Manix, who'd probably never formally trained, only having recently entered ruling of a realm.

Manix cast a spell, hitting Aodhán as he hurled up a shield, deflecting the spell. Energy flew out, striking the ground in a large explosion, the boom echoing. Aodhán pulled together his energy again, cursing his captivity. His reflexes weren't as honed as they'd been years ago. He had to act soon, or Manix would hit with another hex. Aodhán sent a spell toward Manix, who twisted and flew sideways—the charm cast into a cloud, forcing thunder to erupt.

Manix laughed, *~Yer captivity will aid me. Ye are lazy, out of practice in the art of Fae war.~*

Manix flew past Aodhán, his wing clipping his arm, cutting it, *~Yer weakness shall bring about my victory.~*

Aodhán paused as he healed his arm. His gaze flicked to Evie, who lay on the balcony, still as death. He detected her life force, weak but present. Worry for her plagued his mind, but he pushed past it. He needed to focus. He had to win, not only for the realms, but for Evie.

Calling upon his soul, Aodhán built energy again. Manix chuckled as his energy gathered as well. They flung the spell out simultaneously, the force hitting the other as sparks flew from the contact. Manix pushed against Aodhán's power, but Aodhán answered with a force of his own. The contact area sparked again, and energy bolts flew, hitting trees and lighting them on fire. Aodhán flew higher, trying to gain the upper level, a stronger angle, but Manix followed, flying beside him. They twisted and turned as each tried to push against the other to gain a stronger hold. The powerful force between them caused the dizzying trek.

Manix flew close, breaking the connection as Aodhán's spell flew into the clouds. Manix clipped him with his horned tail, sending Aodhán spiraling to the earth. The view of the ocean's water came fast to Aodhán. He hit before he had time to throw up a shield. The impact of the water knocked his breath. As Aodhán sank deeper and deeper, he tried to regain himself. His world tilted and spun as the water pressed in. Aodhán stopped fighting and allowed the comforting presence of its tranquility to wash over him. In that moment, he felt peace. Faith came to him—faith in himself, his people, Evie. No doubt, only faith. *In the absence of doubt, only faith is found.*

Aodhán assembled energy using the water's denseness to muffle his actions. He sensed Manix trying to reach him, but without any of the water's powers, the density diminished Manix's reach.

Aodhán smirked. He collected power and energy to cast his next hex, part faith and water. Aodhán propelled himself toward Manix, gathering the power of water along the way, carrying it toward evil.

With the force of a spell wrapped in water, Aodhán burst from the sea. The energy hit Manix, the water washing over him, pushing him into the ocean. As Aodhán recovered, the dragon flailed in the water, desperate to gain the surface. Aodhán chuckled. It seemed Manix hadn't learned to swim in his dragon form—too bad; they swam well once acclimated to the water.

In Manix's struggle, he flung a spell out. Aodhán sensed its travel—it had no target. The hex flinging wide hit Evie, causing her to jolt and scream.

Aodhán yelled. "No! She's not part of this!"

Manix rose from the rough surf, *~Ye! It's ye who has caused this. Her death will be on yer hands!~*

Manix's wings beat as water dripped from him, and he rose over Aodhán, *~She's all part of this and more. The prophecies intertwine and connect—yet don't. One sees the other's end, while another sees the other's victory.~*

Aodhán froze. Both intertwined? His grandda mentioned nothing of this. Aodhán's eyes shot to Evie, who lay panting as she rolled over, clutching her hands to her chest. Two prophecies? Was this a trick from Manix, from the evil Fae?

Aodhán gathered energy fast, flung a spell, and hit Manix, forcing him to tumble into the sky.

Manix quickly righted.

Aodhán collected more energy and power from faith and goodness, folded over with his love for Evie, forming an impactful spell. He flung it out fast and hit Manix in pulses, one after another. All powered by faith, by the good in Aodhán.

Manix tumbled and hit the earth hard, causing a wave of vibrations in the top layer of vegetation, disrupting the realm. As each pulse hit Manix, he rolled and moaned, pleading to someone. Manix's pleas went unanswered, yet he sent them nonetheless.

Who, who was his savior?

Manix raised his eyes, his gaze connecting with Aodhán's. *~Please save me.~*

Manix's desperation washed over Aodhán. The power of Manix's aura hit him. First, black, indicating evil and dark. With Manix's sigh, the color twisted and morphed from black, fading into red, which meant energetic and fiery. Impulsive, not evil.

Aodhán's eyes went wide. Manix was good, not evil.

Aodhán called over the roar of the wind, the ocean, "Manix, there is good in ye! Stop this battle. End this now!"

****

As Manix tumbled out of control, Evie's statement from the other day echoed in his head, "Trust, Manix. Faith trusts even when plans go against human reason or experience."

Manix hit the ground as Aodhán's spells hit him one after another, tearing at his soul and ripping apart his defenses.

Manix called out to his father, *~Help me!~*

Balor yelled his reply, *~Get up, ye lazy lout!~*

Manix had trusted his father in this quest. Would he abandon him now? Allow him to suffer. Doubts flooded Manix's heart.

Manix raised his eyes, his gaze connecting with Aodhán's. *~Please save me.~*

Goodness filled Manix. He didn't want to kill, didn't want to battle—only to live.

Aodhán's eyes went wide. Fae boy must have sensed he was good, not evil.

Aodhán called over the roar of the wind, the ocean, "Manix, there is good in ye! Stop this battle. End this now!"

Balor roared again, *~Weak! All my sons are weak! The good in ye make ye less than a man!~*

Aodhán paused, and Manix threw a spell, hitting him. Aodhán fell from the sky but caught himself, flying up again.

Manix shook himself and stood as Balor roared in his head again, *~Fail me again, boy, and I'll send ye back where I found ye. Cast ye out, maybe kill ye myself!~*

Memories of the dark cell, the lack of food, and the multiple beatings came to Manix. The memories, still raw after all this time, rocked his soul. *No!*

Manix flung his wings and arms out, collecting energy from all around, pulling in on anything he encountered. He detected a thread he'd not before, not from Aodhán, but another.

Manix sensed Aodhán generate energy for a spell. Manix cast his out, hitting Aodhán, who screamed at the impact.

Balor grunted, *~Good boy.~*

Manix focused on the weak thread of energy. He

followed the slender line to his castle, to Evie on the balcony.

Well, that little bitch. She sent energy to her Fae boy, her dream lover. Jealously washed over Manix as his desire for her pulsed vigorously on him. She was his! His true love, his soul mate—his only. Greed filled him, and jealousy filled him with power.

The force of evil returned to Manix as he chuckled, *~Evie, helping yer Fae boy. We can't have that.~*

He reached out and pulled on her thread of energy. A gem flew from her hands to him, making her cry out.

Manix caught the stone and rotated the gem in his claw. He held it tight, forcing the spell from within out. A lone tear dropped from his tight fist. A tear gem, Aodhán gave Evie a tear gem. Well, not anymore. He twisted his wrist and brought forth the Stone of Doubt. It was time for this battle to end.

Manix pulled on the energy of the realms. Whatever he could find, he harvested for himself, regardless of who or what he hurt. The vegetation around Tor Castle wilted as trees bent over, sapped of their life force. Fomoire people cried out as he drew on their powers. The energy filled him, churned inside, combined with his greed and evil. It was all his for the taking. Balor had promised his rule, and Manix planned to take his due.

Aodhán, it was his fault. He took *her* from him. Evie, his soul mate. It was time for Aodhán to die.

Manix thrust his claw out, casting a spell and wrapping Aodhán in a firm grip of force.

Aodhán's arms clamped to his side, the force gripping him as he cried out.

Balor chuckled. *~Good boy. Yer hate consumes ye!*

Use it now to kill the future Fae king. All the realms will be mine!~

Manix flew in a circle, dragging Aodhán behind, dropping him every so often onto the earth, enjoying the sound of his body hitting the ground. The echo of his body in pain filled his soul. Evie was his, his to take, use, and conquer.

Manix landed in the castle's garden as he flung Aodhán into the sky, keeping him in a tight grip. Manix couldn't lose him now that he had him exactly where he wanted him.

Manix's mind taunted Aodhán, *~Ye had to fuck her, didn't ye? Take the virgin's blood that was mine!~*

Manix's focus returned to Evie, who watched the scene unfold on the balcony. Good. She needed to know who her master was. Let her watch her Fae boy's torture, his mortal death.

Manix returned his focus to Aodhán. He tightened his grip, squeezing the Fae boy.

Aodhán screamed and writhed in agony.

Evie called out from her cage, "Aodhán!"

Balor laughed. *~Do it, boy. Kill him now!~*

Manix gripped the Stone of Doubt in his claw, bringing forth its power and reveling in the surge of energy that washed over him. He combined hate, greed, and jealousy into one ball of energy and sent a stream of power in one line to Aodhán. If he held it long enough, the power would drain the life force of his mortal being, killing him. He'd made the mistake of giving away his immortality, and now he'd pay. Pay for taking what was Manix's.

Balor clapped and shouted, *~That's it! Finally, a son has obeyed my command!~*

As Manix sent the energy hurting Aodhán, he detected a pull on the Stone of Doubt. Then, a hard tug. The gem came free of his claw and shot away. The powerful force stream faded, and Aodhán's limp body fell into the ocean.

****

The world tilted again and again as Fae's powers flew around Evie. Some hit the ground, and some hit Manix or Aodhán. She'd never witnessed a Fae battle, and while it was impressive, it frightened her. The power electrified the ground, the sky, the castle, and even the air.

A bolt hit her, shooting sharp pain through her whole body. Aodhán shouted, but she couldn't make sense of anything. The ringing of her ears took over all thought. She rolled over, holding the teardrop stone closer.

Another power mass built near her. The stone flew from Evie's hand, making her cry out.

She rolled back over, and the scene that met her eyes was out of a nightmare. Manix had Aodhán in a forced grip, holding him tight as he dragged him behind him.

Evie called out from her cage, "Aodhán!"

Aodhán's mind speak came to her, weak but there, *~Evie, stay put. I'll get the Stone of Doubt from Manix.~*

The Stone of Doubt? Of course—the Fae fable, the stone. It had to be what Manix used to generate enough energy to overpower Aodhán, the one Fae with the strongest powers known.

Evie closed her eyes, trying to locate the one thread of power that came from the magic Iona Stone. She had to find the thread of doubt to find the stone.

From Manix, a long power stream shot out, hitting Aodhán, and the world filled with doubt. Manix had it. Evie only needed to lock in on the stone and call it to her. She'd pulled stones to her many times. The magic stone would come to her like all the others.

She focused on Manix's claw, gathered the doubt from around him, and filled her soul. When she had all her mind and soul could handle, she thrust her hand out, calling the Stone of Doubt to her. It nudged but didn't come. She tried again, stronger this time, pouring all she had into the pull. It flew from Manix's claw, landing in her hands.

Manix roared, the dragon's sound rocking the realms with its power. He turned his focus on her, and evil filled the air. She held the Stone of Doubt close as she crawled to her knees.

Manix took to the skies, flying over her. *~Evie, the Stone of Doubt. It is ours to use to control the realms. Come by my side, my sweet. Be my lover, my queen, and we shall rule the realms.~*

Evie rocked, pulling herself up. She faltered but stood tall, gathering all the hate, anger, and frustration with Manix. Folding those feelings within her love, desire, and care for Aodhán.

She glanced at the spot where he'd entered the surf.

She sent a mind speak to Aodhán, *~No doubts, Aodhán. Do not drift. Come back to me.~*

Tears ran down her face with the force of her love and her faith that Aodhán would survive. She had a duty to the Fae. The fable called for a MacDougall to search for a magic Iona Stone, and she must answer the call. For now, she must focus and send Manix to hell and beyond.

Manix chuckled. ~*Tears, Evie? Ye waste yer tears on yer Fae Boy. He is dead.*~

Evie lifted her face, meeting Manix's evil glare. "There is a sacredness in tears. They are not the mark of weakness but of power. The power of tears shall quell any person."

Casting all doubt and using her faith and trust in Aodhán, trust in their love, Evie sent all her energy to Manix in one powerful spell.

A ball of crackling energy flew from her hand, holding the Stone of Doubt, hitting Manix midair. His scream reverberated across the realm. The Fomoire people screamed as one, then fell silent. Manix's body flashed from human to dragon to human. He stretched and twisted like a rubber band, then snapped back into his human form.

Manix's muttered words came to her as his body faded. "The princess gave her soul to the devil to become a swan and fly away, escaping her capture. But her heart the warlock kept for him alone. She might be free but never be able to love again."

As he let out one long, painful wail, his body disappeared from the sky.

Energy sapped, Evie collapsed and lay on the balcony. The black obsidian rock morphed into sandstone as her vision blurred. Her breath came short, and her mind numbed. She sighed once and closed her eyes, too weak to sense herself anymore.

Back in her dream, Evie wrapped herself against her unicorn as a light from above called, like her ghosts. Friends and family long gone reached for her, and she relaxed in their embrace.

Chapter 17

Aodhán shot from the ocean, breaking the surface as Manix faded from view. It'd taken him a considerable amount of time to regain himself. He'd used the water's power to fuel his.

He caught the last whispered words from Manix. "The princess gave her soul to the devil to become a swan and fly away, escaping her capture. But her heart the warlock kept for him alone. She might be free but never be able to love again." As Manix's body faded from the realm, so did his power and soul. Wherever he'd gone, it was not of the Fae or human realm that Aodhán could sense.

Evie's call to him rang loud in his mind, the last she'd spoken. ~*No doubts. Aodhán, do not drift. Stay with me.*~

His gaze flew to the balcony.

Her body folded and crumpled as she still clutched the Stone of Doubt.

Whatever had happened here, Evie came out the victor. Echoes of the battle remained, and Aodhán locked on them, replaying the scene before the energy waves faded.

Manix had taunted Evie, but she'd found the stone, gathered energy, and sent all she had to Manix, sending him beyond the realms. Aodhán felt the Fomoire people sigh as one, the awareness that Manix had left them a relief to the kingdom.

She did it, not him. Her powers saved them and cast Manix into the unknown, restoring the Fomoire kingdom to the Fae realm, but at what cost?

Aodhán's focus went to the balcony. "Evie."

He flew to her as Tor Castle morphed from its black, forbidding image in the Fae realm to the beautiful sandstone of the human realm.

He took her in his arms, her cold body sending chills over him. He reached for her life force and found only a thread. The gods called her soul to come to them.

Aodhán held his true love to his breast. He placed his hand over her heart, trying a heart meld. He knew the Fae forbade it, but he tried it anyway—nothing. He tried a spell, one of love cast upon Evie to bring her back, but still nothing. Desperation filled his heart.

Aodhán roared, "No! This is not her fate. Not our destiny!"

His ma's voice, Brigid, echoed in his mind, "Tempting fate, tempting the wrath of destiny. Son, ye play with powers greater than even ye."

Was this the price to pay? Evie's life taken once they'd found each other again. Not if he could help it.

He gathered her closer, gripping her hand that held the Stone of Doubt, as tears filled his eyes. "A vow. I made a vow of undying love to this woman! A vow I pledged to keep through all eternity!"

Her life force faded as her body grew light, a sign she transferred to the holy realm.

Tears streamed down his face as he screamed again, "No! I gave my oath, my immortality, to this woman. I call upon the gods. My immortality is hers!"

He gripped the Stone of Doubt as he yelled into the

sky, "My immortality is hers! The vow I made was for her! The vow is hers!"

The stone warmed, then glowed. A star burst into the sky and hovered over them. Aodhán sat transfixed. The star pulsed once, then again. Soon, it beat with the rhythm of his heart.

Aodhán held Evie close. "Forever, my soul is kept in this stone. A part of my blood, a part of my bone. A piece of myself I give to thee. A part of my soul for all eternity."

The star glowed brighter and flew into Evie's chest. It pulsed and blazed, then faded.

Aodhán sat holding a still Evie. He took a breath, then another, waiting, praying the gods gifted them with mercy.

He whispered, "Evie, don't leave. We are one."

****

Evie sensed a warming, then the sensation of being lifted. Strong arms held her as the light and her friends and family faded.

Someone yelled from a distance. It echoed in her head. Heat radiated from her hand. A buzzing filled her head. Her body felt thrust through space and time. She stopped, cradled in someone's arms. Not someone, Aodhán's

Aodhán called to her from afar, "Evie, come back to me."

Her breath came as one, a huge gulp as her eyes shot open to the sight of Aodhán holding her as tears ran down his face.

She gulped once, then again as her breath came under control.

Aodhán's expression of astonishment almost made

her smile, but his tears tore at her heart. "Tears? Why tears?"

Aodhán hiccupped and sat them up. "Ye almost died, Evie. I had to call ye back."

She glanced about. "Manix, he is gone?"

Aodhán nodded. "Aye, ye sent him away, but to where I do not know."

Her hand came up, holding the Stone of Doubt. "The stone, ye got it?"

Aodhán wrapped his hand around hers, holding the stone. "Not me. Ye, Evie."

She glanced at him. "How?"

"The gods gave ye my gift of immortality. The one I vowed to the wrong woman by mistake. My gift saved yer life."

Evie sat for a moment as doubts plagued her mind.

Aodhán took the Stone of Doubt from her, and all her doubts faded, yet one remained.

She fisted her hand as she raised her eyes to him. "Aodhán, Manix said something as he faded, a spell, I think. I fear my heart is the warlock's to keep, like in Manix's play, but the dragon's now."

Aodhán held her close and brushed a kiss across her lips. "Impossible. Ye gave yer heart to me so many years ago. I've protected it with my soul and will keep it safe for all eternity."

****

Months later, Evie strolled hand in hand with Aodhán toward the Chapel in the Woods at Dunstaffnage Castle—home. The wind blew cold as she tucked the Stone of Doubt farther into her coat. Her mother and father kept pace beside them, also holding hands. Evie took a deep breath, sensing the power of each couple's love flow. Love—she'd found her love, her Fae boy. She glanced at Aodhán's profile, admiring his long jawline and regal nose. The wind moved again, shifting his long blond hair. His ear peeked out, curved, not pointed. Mortal, he chose to become mortal to live a lifetime with her. His love and devotion humbled her.

Aodhán glanced at her, winked, and kissed the back of her hand. He must have read her mind. Mortal, yet with Fae's powers, like her. She smiled, masking her thoughts as she'd done so many times with her brother. Would their daughter be the same? She touched her belly, hoping so.

Her da huffed from beside her, "I hate it when ye both do that *mind speak* like yer brother. I hear yer whispers."

Aodhán chuckled as Evie turned to him. "We did not, Da. I promise."

Bree sighed as they continued to the chapel. "Leave the love birds be, Colin." She smirked at her true love. "There was one day we were the same, you know."

They arrived at the closed chapel doors.

Colin took her ma in his arms. "Aye, and we still are." He kissed her full on the mouth, making Evie grin. One day, she'd be just like them, in love over and over in so many ways.

Aodhán squeezed her hand once, a sign that he'd heard her thoughts.

Colin opened the chapel doors and then stepped back. He spoke lowly to her ma, "They grow up, yer wee bugs."

They stood there a moment as the building seemed to take a breath.

Evie drew the Stone of Doubt from her coat and held it to her da. "Well, it's time. The stone must go to the Fae realm like all the others."

Colin took her ma in his arms and held her as he spoke, "The fable called for ye, Evie. 'Tis ye who should place the gem in its resting place. Not me."

Her da turned with her ma and strode back down the path to the castle, leaving Evie with her mouth hanging open.

Her ma called over her shoulder, "Evie dear, make sure to close the chapel doors when you finish. The wind's picking up. Might be a storm blowing in."

Evie stood holding the magic Iona stone as she called after her parents, "I don't know what to do! How do I get the stone back to the Fae?"

Her da wrapped his arm around her ma as they continued down the path.

She turned to Aodhán, who covered his mouth with his hand, holding in his laughter.

Evie marched past him into the nave. "Not funny, Aodhán. I've never done this before."

She stopped at the front and turned as he followed her inside the space, their steps echoing a little. "Hey, this mortal world is all new to me. I haven't the foggiest idea what to do."

He came to her and took her in his arms. "Except this." He bent and kissed her lips softly at first. Then, he took her in his arms, kissing her till she lost track of her thoughts.

He lifted his head. "Now, that's better."

Aodhán took her hand and led her to the pew, pulling her next to him. "Let's sit a while. Maybe something will come to us."

Evie followed his lead, hoping he knew what he was about. She sat with him and stared at the stained-glass window above the altar. The cross lit up in the day's light, casting the image in yellow sunlight on the floor. The sun's rays illuminated the dust particles in the air. The wind blew around the chapel again, and the dust specs danced, reminding her of fairies—a grin formed on Evie's face. The last time she was in the chapel was when she first left for college, and the Dunstaffnage ghost visited her with another woman in tow. Evie glanced about, at first not sensing her. When her gaze returned to the altar, the ghost floated there smiling. It was the second time the ghost smiled at her. The sun shone brighter, and the apparition faded.

Evie settled back, and Aodhán took her hand in his. They sat for some time, the quiet comforting, his company soothing.

Aodhán sighed. "This has been quite a journey, Evie. From years ago, to now. Finding one another again."

Evie turned to him. "Aye, it has."

Aodhán lifted her hand to his lips, kissing the back. "I am delighted to have traveled it." He kissed her hand again. "And all ones we shall travel in our future."

Evie's mind flooded with doubt. Her concern rose. Aodhán reached over and took the Stone of Doubt from her. Doubt faded from Evie's mind and heart.

Aodhán flipped the gemstone in the air. "Ye can't hold it so long. It's evil." He folded it to his chest, the stone disappearing.

Evie nodded. "This journey, I've learned so much." She sighed. "After floundering, I realized doubt isn't the opposite of faith. It's a part of it. And when I embraced that, well, my doubt became something that helped my faith grow."

Aodhán smiled. "Faith is a powerful emotion."

Evie grinned. "Aye, but trust is stronger. Faith trusts even when plans go against human reason or experience." She glanced away. "I tried to explain it to Manix, but he never understood."

Aodhán squeezed her hand once, and her attention returned to him as he spoke, "Faith is often seen as the opposite of doubt. But that perspective needs to be flipped. The opposite of faith is certainty. Where there is certainty, there is no room for doubt. My certainty is my love for ye, Evie."

As he bent and kissed her lips, energy gathered, and the world tilted slightly, like when Brigid appeared. Maybe it was the morning sickness she'd started to feel these days. As he ended the kiss, awareness came over Evie. Someone was with them in the chapel.

Aodhán smirked, keeping his eyes on Evie's as he spoke, "Hello, Mother."

Evie gasped and turned, searching for her mentor. Brigid floated above the altar in her wee Fae form, her iridescent wings fluttering fast.

Brigid landed, sitting on the table before them. "Ah, my favored student and my son. Ye both look to have weathered the trails quite well."

Evie stood, wavered in dizziness as Aodhán jolted and took her in his arms.

Brigid raised an eyebrow. "So soon, son? Ye haven't wasted yer time in the human realm. When will my grandson arrive?"

Evie gasped as Aodhán sat her back down with him. "A few more months. The mother has yet to admit as much to the father, but we men know these things."

Evie swatted his arm. "I was going to surprise ye!"

Aodhán kissed her. "And ye have."

Brigid snorted as she folded her arms. "A child out of wedlock."

Aodhán twisted his hand, and a ring appeared. The teardrop gem glinted in the sun's rays mounted on a golden setting.

Evie sputtered, "I thought Manix destroyed my tear gem."

Aodhán placed it on her finger. "Manix cannot touch what is between us. He is not more powerful than true love."

Aodhán held her hand as he whispered, "Be my wife in this life and the next."

Tears gathered in Evie's eyes as she whimpered, "Aye."

Brigid sighed. "Well, task one, done." She held her hand out to her son. Aodhán flicked his wrist, and the Stone of Doubt flew up, suspended. Brigid flicked her wrist, and the stone spun. Faster and faster till it rose into the ray of sunlight, it flashed once, then again in a brilliant spark of bright yellow light. When Evie blinked, the stone wasn't there. She glanced about, wondering where the stone had gone, not finding anything out of place. She turned, and her eyes landed on Aodhán.

His knowing expression met hers as he spoke, "It's better if ye don't know where they are. We still have the prophecy to fulfill, my love."

Evie tilted her head. "We do? It's not over?"

As Aodhán shook his head, Brigid flew high and twirled her hand as sparks circled her. "Aye, that and a wedding to plan. Guests to invite, flowers to gather, a dress fit for a bride of the future king of the Fae." As she faded from sight, she called out, "So much to do and so little time."

Evie blinked as what Brigid said registered.

Her eyes flew to Aodhán, "A wedding in the Fae realm? Really?"

Aodhán nodded and kissed her. "Aye, my love."

Chapter 18

Evie stood in a private bedroom in Broemere castle in the Fae realm. Her dress flowed about her as she turned one way, then another, admiring it in the mirror. The fabric glittered in the sunlight from the expansive window. It looked like organza but flowed softer, like silk.

Brigid stood behind her in her human-size form. Her reflection in the mirror showed her wide smile.

Their eyes connected as Brigid spoke, "The overdress I made after Aodhán arrived." She approached and fingered the delicate fabric. "I knew he'd find his true love in the human realm. His mate and match for all eternity." Evie teared up as she turned to face her mentor, her future mother-in-law. Brigid hugged her.

Bree, her mother, spoke from behind them, "Now, no tears. We all agreed. Plus, our makeup would run."

Bree approached with her crown and veil. "Brigid and I made this for you, daughter."

Her mother set the most exquisite crown on her head. A maid had braided her hair and weaved glass beads and pearls through the brown tresses. The crown was silver, woven together in an intricate pattern resembling vines. Pearls and clear glass beads winked from the crown. At the front was a teardrop pearl the size of her thumb.

Bree placed it on Evie's head, shifting it till it fit where the pearl hung over her forehead. "This, my dear daughter, combines Fae and MacDougall."

Her ma and Brigid exchanged a glance.

Brigid fingered the large pearl. "The pearl is from yer auntie Ainslie's crown."

Evie gasped. "Really? From the Viking time?"

Brigid nodded. "Aye, used many a time over again over the years. Kept here in the Fae realm for ye at Ainslie's request." Evie teared up and took a deep breath, trying to keep the flood at bay.

Her mother fluttered the veil. "The veil was mine from when I married yer da."

Brigid grinned as all three gazes met in the reflection. "The silver crown was mine when I married Asmund, Aodhán's father."

Brigid hiccupped as she spoke, "A symbol of the blending of our families and something ye will keep for yer daughter's ceremony."

Evie blinked back tears and adjusted the crown to ensure it didn't fall off her head.

Kat burst through the door, almost hitting it before it faded into an opening. "Evie, ye won't believe what the throne room looks like!" Her dress, also in the Fae organza fabric, glittered light blue.

The dress flowed in motion even after an enthusiastic Kat stopped beside Evie. "The flowers are all white and pink. Gardenias, bougainvillea, and roses all intertwined with ivy." She sighed audibly. "It's the wedding of my dreams!"

Evie caught Brigid's eye in the mirror, who winked at her.

Kat spun and landed on the bed of clouds, causing

the billowy puffs to fly out. "Oh, did ye see the Fae people?" She sat up, her curls bouncing. "Aodhán's cousin Ceallach, named after a son of Poseidon and Kalyke whom his father made invulnerable to weapons!" She fell back again, puffs flying up. "Dark long hair with his regal nose." She sighed. "He is built like a bodybuilder. He's so dreamy!"

Brigid smirked as she spoke, "Aye, well, ye and all of the women in the Fae realm feel the same way about Ceallach."

Bree stepped toward Kat. "Kathryn, you must not wrinkle the gown. And your hair, don't muss it!" Kat sat up, shrugging. "Aw, Mrs. Mac, it'll be okay. Brigid can wave her hand and fix it."

Brigid grunted, "Not if ye keep fouling up my work!"

Many large bells rang, echoing throughout the kingdom. Brigid stood tall. "It's time. They call everyone to the wedding." She waved all the women together. "Come hold hands, and I'll shift us there."

Kat jumped up and grabbed Evie's hand. "Oh, this part is so much fun! I've traveled through a portal that shifted in space and time. Now a Fae wedding!"

Evie squeezed her BFF's hand. "Aye, ye have, but remember, ye can't tell any tall tales of this. That's when the Fae erase yer memory."

Bree took their hands, and Brigid took Kat's other. "Aye, these memories are kept close to the heart."

Evie closed her eyes as the world tilted a bit, the sign they shifted. Kat giggled, and Bree shushed her. The world righted, and Evie opened her eyes to her ma's smiling face as the other women moved away to their places for the ceremony.

Bree held her hand tightly and kissed her cheek. "I love you with all my heart. You found your true love as I have. I am so happy for you." Her ma patted Evie's flat belly. "And your growing family!"

Bree turned, passing Evie's hand to her da's. Colin MacDougall stood tall in his full highland regalia of historical dress complete. Thankfully, he left his broadsword behind. The Fae forbade human weapons in the Fae realms.

Her da wordlessly took her hand, placed it on his arm, and turned them to the entrance to the throne room. Kat was right. Evie spied the white and pink flowers intertwined with ivy through the gilded gates. Gardenias, bougainvillea, and roses covered nearly every column in the grand room. Rows upon rows of people sat facing the cliff's window overlooking Broemere ocean and the setting sun beyond. It indeed was a dream wedding.

Her da spoke lowly near Evie's ear, "So, this new boy ye date. He's a good man?"

Evie nudged him with her elbow. "Da, ye know full and well who Aodhán is. Ye questioned him for days before ye permitted this union."

Her da chuckled. "Aye, I did. Argued with Dagda over it as well." He sighed. "A Fae as my son-in-law." He huffed, "And that damn sprite's boy as well. They do this to plague me."

Evie sighed. "Da…"

He turned to her and brushed his finger over her cheek. "Does he make ye happy, daughter?"

Evie teared up. "Very much so, Da."

Her da turned to the doorway. "That's good to hear. I'd hate to have to lay him low."

Evie gasped. "Da!"

Her da mumbled, "Taking advantage of my wee bug, getting her pregnant before the wedding."

Evie elbowed him again. "Hey, I did the math. Ye did the same!"

The doors opened, and the music began, saving her da from having to answer.

Her regard went to the floor as she said a short prayer for the beginning of the next part of her life.

When her eyes rose, she met Aodhán's. His eyes glowed, and a slow smile spread across his face. As her da walked her down the aisle, Evie knew her destiny was at hand. She married her Fae boy, her true love.

When they arrived at the altar, Dagda, the King of the Tuatha Dé Danann, stood ready to preside over the ceremony. It wasn't until this moment that she noticed the man, Ceallach, beside Aodhán. His dark looks and large size made him forbidding. To her right stood Kat and another of Aodhán's cousins, Athea, dressed in the same gown as Kat. As she passed, she noted that Ewan and Doug, both in Highland kilts and not their typical pirate garb, sat in the front row beside her mother. She had huffed a laugh, recalling her brother arguing that he should be allowed to wear whatever historical fashion he wanted since they were in the Fae realm. He'd lost the argument with their ma, as he always did. Beside the boys sat Marie and John MacArthur, dressed in historical highland fashion with a wide-eyed Mrs. A beside them. She couldn't invite all the humans she wanted to, and that was fine—a wedding with her family. It was a ceremony of a human wedding combined with that of Fae soul bonding.

Dagda cleared his throat, and her attention returned

to him as he spoke, "Who gives the bride away?"

Her da shifted, holding her hand in his. "Laird Colin Roderick MacDougall gives Evie Emily MacDougall to Aodhán of the Tuatha Dé Danann."

Evie teared up, knowing giving her hand away meant much more than a mere passing. It meant she was no longer his little girl but a grown woman. Her tears faded when her hand contacted Aodhán's, and she glanced up at his smiling face. Her future lay out before her, and happiness filled her soul.

Her da wrapped his hands around theirs, squeezed them once, and then let them go. He stepped down and sat beside her ma, Bree, and they took each other's hands and smiled at Evie.

When she turned back to Aodhán, he winked at her.

Kat stepped up and giggled as she handed them each the other's ring.

Dagda spoke for all to hear, "They shall exchange rings in the tradition of humans. The circle, a symbol of everlasting love." Aodhán slid Evie's tear drop gem ring on her finger, and with it was a gold band. She, in turn, slid a thick gold band on Aodhán's. They held hands as they gazed at each other.

Ceallach stepped up, his expression serious as he handed the Fae's symbol of commitment to Aodhán. Aodhán explained that they were immortal necklaces, symbols, and enchanted stones held within, representing the bonding of souls for eternity. She'd glimpsed it once when he gave it to the maid.

Aodhán's thoughts came to her. ~*Evie, please only think of this moment.*~ She blushed as he took her necklace from Ceallach.

The pendant glittered in the sunlight and held the sign of eternity on top of ivy leaves. Over that sat a five-pointed star made of clear Fae crystal. Aodhán had explained it as the most powerful gem in the Fae realm. The power within had held his immortality. The only item he could give to anyone to form a bond lasting for eternity. The power he'd given her when he saved her.

He placed it around her neck, bending near her ear to close the clasp. He whispered as he brushed a kiss on her ear, "For my true love."

When he stood back, he spoke the Fae vows loud enough for all to hear, "Forever, my soul is kept in this stone. A part of my blood, a part of my bone. A piece of myself I give to thee. A part of my soul for all eternity."

She turned to Aodhán's cousin, who smiled as he handed her Aodhán's necklace, recently restored by the gods. Aodhán bent down as Evie placed the necklace around him. When she did the clasp, the metal fused, and she blinked.

When Aodhán rose, he winked at her. "They will stay on forever."

Evie took a deep breath; her vow was next. She repeated the Fae vow. When she finished, the hall erupted in cheers. Aodhán took her in his arms and kissed her deeply.

Dagda yelled, "Joined they are in this realm and the next!"

Many wished them well, including her friends and parents, plus Dagda and Aodhán's cousins.

Brigid came forward to give her wishes. She hugged Evie long and gave her a short squeeze at the end like her parents did.

When Brigid turned to Aodhán, she held him at

arm's length. "Well, son, ye did it. Changed the outcome of yer destiny." She patted his cheek. "Was it worth the price?"

Aodhán grinned. "A lifetime with my true love. Aye, mother it was."

Brigid nudged his shoulder. "Go on with ye, son. Have yer fun in the human realm. The Fae will be here."

Aodhán turned to Evie and kissed her. "The girl of my dreams, my true love, and the woman of my soul. I love ye."

Evie beamed. "My Fae boy, the man of my dreams and my true love. I love ye."

Aodhán held her close. "Together for all eternity."

Epilogue

Evie waddled and eased her very pregnant body on the couch in their flat in Edinburgh. As Evie and Aodhán took over the first one, Ewan, Doug, and Kat had moved to another. Evie liked the original flat, and Kat wanted a new place to decorate as her own. The boys had gone along with it for convenience.

Evie sighed as she set her swollen feet up on the arm of the couch. Any day now, she'd have their baby—a girl. Evie sensed her soul daily. She knew the feisty one within would come popping out screaming with life, and Evie couldn't wait to meet her. She and Aodhán agreed to call her Annie after Ainslie, Evie's favored auntie who stayed in the Viking times for true love. Evie joked that Annie must be a Viking. Her kicking was so strong.

Aodhán banged more pans in the kitchen as a burnt smell filled the flat. He cursed again, making Evie giggle. Learning to cook as a human was Aodhán's latest project. That and his job as a tour guide for that wizarding school tour through the kirkyard. His Fae powers made his faked sleight-of-hand tricks a favorite among the tourists, and the tour company kept his schedule full. Recently, he got a promotion to training recruits.

Aodhán cursed again, and Evie called out, "Chinese takeaway sounds perfect, honey!"

A grumble came from the kitchen, "I'll get this right, even if it kills me."

Evie glanced at the coffee table where a stack of magazines sat. They were the *Photographic Journalism Magazine of Scotland*'s recent edition featuring her photo of the famed ghost, Maggie Dickson, Evie's celebrated success. Maggie was an infamous character in Edinburgh's history and Evie's best ghost friend who stayed around a pub named after her in the Garden District of Edinburgh. In the past, they'd hung her just outside the very building, and her family thought her dead until they got halfway home. Maggie sat up, scaring her relatives and all around. Evie never understood why her spirit hadn't transitioned on. She'd lived an entire life after, married, had kids, and died a happy woman. After the wedding, Maggie worked hard gathering energy, and they'd been able to capture a selfie of them together outside the pub where Evie worked until recently.

Evie finally had to give up waitressing. It helped her decision when her boss, Hal, insisted after she recently found fame. She could only be a guest there, never a worker again. After the selfie, Maggie bid a quick goodbye, saying that her time between the realms and her task was complete. The sky opened in a bright light as Maggie's husband and children called her home. Evie still teared up about it, or maybe that was the hormones from being pregnant.

Another pot banged in the kitchen, followed by another of Aodhán's curses.

Evie shifted as a pain cramped her belly, then traveled around her lower back. "Aodhán, ye think my brother and Doug still hop back in time with the pirate ship?"

Her belly cramped again, and Aodhán ran into the room. "Evie, yer brother is the last of my concerns!" Evie rolled over and stood.

Water gushed from between her legs as Aodhán cried out, "Evie, it's Annie, our daughter! She comes!"

****

Doug shouted, "She comes!"

When they came closer, Captain Low shouted, "Hard to port!"

Ewan flicked his wrist, signaling One-eyed Joe, who pulled hard on the wheel. *The Faithful* swung wider to their starboard. Ewan's replica galleon, outfitted with a more modern steering system and a wider rudder, turned quicker than the eighteenth-century frigate barreling at them.

When the jibbooms crossed, Doug yelled, "Guns at the ready!" Their gunner ports opened as the roar of rolling guns rattled *The Faithful*.

Fireman Flint yelled, "Tine!" *Fire. The Faithful's* guns roared as the vessels came side by side. As the ships posed in midrise on a small wave, multiple booms rocked Ewan's eardrums, silencing his mind for a millisecond. The boats moved again, and splinters of wood flew off Low's ship, *The Fancy,* as the roar of men's howls rang in the air. The vessel continued passing as sailors topside shot at one another.

Low's gun ports opened on his port side. Damn, that was a fast turnaround.

Low shouted, "Fire." The roar of cannons boomed again, taking out sections of Ewan's ship.

Flint rallied with another answer to the volley, Low's precious ship, *The Fancy,* taking another brutal hit.

Through the smoke, Ewan spotted Low, who raised his fist, yelling, "You will regret this! Blackbeard's ghost? Not! I see you clear as day! The warlock will find you!"

Ewan saluted him. "I do hope he does. Tell him the jewels will make a perfect addition to my collection!"

Low followed Ewan's passing with a sharp eye.

Ewan called back, "Why so many? Does yer sponsor need extra adornment to look pretty?"

The cannons drowned out Low's response as Ewan spied the woman again, standing at the bow alone—the same as she had the last few ships he'd robbed. No one else seemed to see her, and the battle raged on without hitting her.

Her bright red hair spread about her head as the wind tossed it. Her cream-colored skin glowed, and when their eyes came in contact, a blush rose. She had Fae eyes, a brilliant white-blue that shone on their own. A siren she was, the woman from his dreams. Someone no one else saw but Ewan. She took his breath away each time, touching his soul and making his heart beat harder. Butterflies erupted in his belly.

Doug stepped in front of him, breaking the spell. The sounds of battle rushed back into his awareness like a freight train.

Doug yelled, "Ewan, ye must shift us before the ship breaks up! We've taken the plunder and freed the slaves. It's time for Blackbeard's ghost to disappear."

Cannon fire broke apart pieces of his prized ship. Doug was right. It was past time to disappear.

Ewan gathered energy, concentrating on the Chapel in the Woods. He thrust his hand out, opening the portal, and sent a ball of energy through. He called the ship and all who were within forward in time.

The ship swirled, and the world tilted as Doug cheered. The vessel flew through space and time, popping out of the chapel door and landing in the loch beyond Dunstaffnage Castle, rocking a bit from the force. He and Doug tumbled on the chapel floor, coming to rest and lying on their backs. The crew Ewan knew faded, spirits brought back to serve him that dissipated with his spell. Ewan lay there a moment, allowing his body and mind to rest. Doug did as well, as their breaths echoed in the empty nave.

Boot steps sounded, and before Ewan could rise, his da's angry face appeared over him, upside down. "About damn time ye returned! I've waited half a day for ye to get yer pirate ass home!"

His da strode away, calling out as he neared the chapel door, "Both ye sorry mongrels, get yer asses into the study! And make that scraggly beard disappear, Ewan!"

Ewan sat up, waving at his chin, the long beard fading as Doug stood. "Laird Mac, it's just a bit of fun, that's all!"

Colin Roderick MacDougall stopped, straightened his back as if to strike, and turned slowly.

His angry countenance was one Ewan rarely witnessed. "Just a bit of fun, Douglas MacArthur? Just a bit of fun?"

His da fisted his hands. "Yer pirate games have gone too far!" He slashed his hand to the side. "The study, now!" The last he bellowed, echoing beyond the chapel.

Ewan stood, knowing his da's wrath was not easily

risen when disciplining his children, except when…
"What, Da? What has happened?" Ewan and Evie had
gotten away with so much as kids. Colin had grunted
most of the time, yet others applauded their skills.

His da pointed a finger at him. "A Fae fable has
shown itself. That's what's happened!" He strode to
Ewan and pointed his finger, hitting his broad chest,
jabbing as he yelled, "The Stone of Faith!"

Ewan blinked. The Stone of Faith fable had two
stories they knew of, both including the Stone of Lust.
One in the *Fae Fable Book* told of a greedy man and an
island sinking with his ma on it with "the maiden" and
no ending. Then there was his Auntie Ainslie's version
told to her by his grandma, the story of a female Viking
warrior, like Auntie Ainslie. As children, when Brigid
had him and his sister learn all the fables, Faith didn't
have one of its own.

Ewan tilted his head. "Ainslie's story or the other
one of the island and treasure?"

His da folded his arms as he growled his answer.
"The island of treasure." His da leaned forward till their
noses nearly touched. "And it's not about yer ma. It's
one of its own, and the damn thing has an ending!" He
turned and strode out of the chapel.

Ewan blinked. "The Stone of Faith has a fable?"

A word about the author...

Margaret Izard is a multi-award-winning author of historical fantasy and paranormal romance novels. She spent her early years through college to adulthood dedicated to dance, theater, and performing. Over the years, she developed a love for great storytelling in different mediums. She does not waste a good story, be it movement, the spoken, or the written word. She discovered historical romance novels in middle school, which combined her passion for romance, drama, and fantasy. She writes exciting plot lines, steamy love scenes and always falls for a strong male with a soft heart. She lives in Houston, Texas, with her husband and adult triplets and loves to hear from readers.

You can email me at:
info@margaretizardauthor.com
www.margaretizardauthor.com